Clive Sinclair was born in London in 1948 and educated at the universities of East Anglia and California at Santa Cruz. His stories, interviews and articles have been published in *Encounter*, *New Review*, *Quarto*, *London Magazine*, *Penthouse*, *Transatlantic Review*, *The Year's Best Horror Stories*, *Club International*, *Lillit* and *Firebird I* (Penguin, 1982). His first novel, *Bibliosexuality*, was published in 1973, and his previous collection of stories, *Hearts of Gold* (Penguin, 1982), won the Somerset Maugham Award in 1981. He was also awarded a Bicentennial Arts Fellowship in 1980, as a result of which he spent a year writing and teaching in America. Half the stories in this collection were written there. He has also written a biographical–critical study of Isaac Bashevis Singer and Israel Joshua Singer entitled *The Brothers Singer* (1982).

CLIVE SINCLAIR

BEDBUGS

A KING PENGUIN
PUBLISHED BY PENGUIN BOOKS

Penguin Books Ltd, Harmondsworth, Middlesex, England
Penguin Books, 625 Madison Avenue, New York, New York 10022, U.S.A.
Penguin Books Australia Ltd, Ringwood, Victoria, Australia
Penguin Books Canada Ltd, 2801 John Street, Markham, Ontario, Canada L3R 1B4
Penguin Books (N.Z.) Ltd, 182–190 Wairau Road, Auckland 10, New Zealand

First published by Allison & Busby 1982
Published in Penguin Books 1983

Made and printed in Great Britain by
Richard Clay (The Chaucer Press) Ltd, Bungay, Suffolk
Filmset in Monophoto Ehrhardt by
Northumberland Press Ltd, Gateshead

CONTENTS

ACKNOWLEDGEMENTS

Half these stories were written in Santa Cruz, California, while I was the recipient of a Bicentennial Arts Fellowship. Thanks are also due to the editors of the following magazines where several of the stories first appeared: *Encounter* ('Bedbugs', 'Genesis', 'Ashkenazia'), *London Magazine* ('Tzimtzum'), *Quarto* ('The Incredible Case of the Stack o' Wheats Murders', 'Somewhere over the Rainbow', 'Svoboda'), *Jewish Chronicle Literary Review* ('Tsatske'). 'America' was first published in the Penguin anthology *Firebird 1*.

The lines on pages 12 and 16 are taken from 'Louse Hunting' in *Poems* by Isaac Rosenberg, Heinemann, London, 1922. Those on page 86 come from 'Letter to My Wife' in *Forced March: Selected Poems* by Miklós Radńoti, translated by Clive Wilmer and George Gömöri, Carcanet, Manchester, 1979.

For
Fran and Seth

Bedbugs

During the night I have a vision of bedbugs in congress. A concrescence of male and female. The polluted mass pulsates, masculine organs pullulate, grow into dangerous spikes that, blinded by passion, miss the proffered orifices and stab deep into the soft bellies of their consorts. While I thus dream, my blood is sucked and the satiated bugs, too bloated to return to their hiding places, excrete their waste upon the sheets and make their getaway. When I awake I observe the telltale black stains and become conscious of new islands of itchiness erupting upon my body. Life has taken a turn for the better for the dispossessed bedbugs, homeless since the demolition of the ancient slums, with the construction of the concrete college. Here at last the flat-bodied bugs have found sanctuary in the snug crevices, and plenty of food in the beds, even during the long summer vacation when the abandoned beds are filled by foreign students and their teachers – the former having come to Cambridge to improve their English, the latter to improve their finances. I am among the latter.

Some weeks previously I had been telephoned by a director of Literature & Linguistics Ltd, hitherto unknown, and been offered a job as a tutor at their Cambridge Summer School, held annually in the vacated university. He was frank. He said that they had been let down at the last minute and that someone had given him my name; he apologized for the short notice and inquired if I knew anything about the poets of the Great War, the course set by the deserter, for which books had already been purchased and despatched to the students; he added that these students tended to be young, German, intelligent, fluent and – with a chuckle – female; he said by way of conclusion that Literature & Linguistics Ltd was a reputable company and that the salary was equally respectable. I promised to let him know the following day.

Here was irony! Teaching First World War poetry to Germans, who had cut short the careers of most of the poets. Being Jewish I also felt a more personal thin-skinned irony. But was such irony justified? Neither I nor the students were even born in the days of the Third Reich, so could I blame them for the fact that had their parents proved victorious I would never have been born at all? Easily. Then what made me take the position? Money? Of course. But even more persuasive was Isaac Rosenberg. On account of a little-known biographical detail: his affair with my grandmother. He was ten and she was seven. They kissed one fine afternoon outside the Rosenbergs' house in Stepney, a few doors down from my great-grandfather's greengrocery. Furthermore, when Rosenberg decided to enlist he ran away from home and joined a bantam battalion in Bury St Edmunds. You can see his barracks from our bedroom window. The grotesque red-brick pastiche of a castle looms over me as I call the director to announce my acceptance. I do not mention that I have renamed the course Rosenberg's Revenge.

However, the German girls completely disarm me. They are charming, receptive and funny. Above all they seem so innocent. Our first class began in a tentative way, polite, giggly, until one of the girls demanded to know why we were studying such poetry.

'The concerns of the poets are out of date, they do not mean anything to us,' she said, 'especially since we are mostly girls here and not interested in war one bit. So why do you make us read about these horrible things?'

Other girls snorted, to be interpreted as derisive. In that parallel course running in my head, Rosenberg's Revenge, I rubbed the cow's nose in Nazi atrocities, but in our Cambridge classroom I was patient, persuasive. I did not mention the pink stain on her neck which I took to be a love bite, sign of her preoccupations.

'Why? Because the poetry transcends its environment,' I said. 'War becomes the inspiration. A source of destruction, but also creation. A paradox to contemplate. The proximity of death added to the intensity of the poet. Their minds were concentrated wonderfully.'

My allies moved in to attack. Women not interested in war? What nonsense! War involves everybody. My enemy was routed, isolated, leaving the rest of us clear to commence the course. In that introductory meeting, relationships were established, and I was pleased to note that foremost among my supporters was the most attractive girl in the room. Vanity also is an inspiration.

There are two tutors for the twenty students: myself for literature, the other for linguistics, with composition shared. Although Bury St Edmunds is only thirty miles from Cambridge I am expected to sleep in the college, since my duties include evening entertainment. Tonight my colleague is giving a lecture on phonemes, freeing me to telephone my wife. As I listen to the ringing tone I consider the fact that while each peal is identical, subsequent conversation gives it a retrospective value; from phony, wrong number, to euphony for a lover.

'Hello, love,' says my wife, 'miss me?'

'Lots,' I say.

So our catechism continues, a pleasant exchange of self-confidences, until I realize with alarm that my answers are counterfeit. I am not thinking about her. I do not miss her. I am a liar. Second sight suddenly reveals this peccadillo as prophetic and I foresee the wreck of our marriage. Doubtless this is a romantic fallacy to be dismissed as easily as the psychosomatic cramp that has gripped my stomach. What harm can there be in euphemism if it makes her happy?

'Sleep well,' says my wife, 'sweet dreams.'

But the belly-ache won't go away. Back in my room I stretch upon the bed. My room is modernistic, without extraneous matter; for example there are no handles on the drawers, just holes for fingers to pull them open. Being double the room is a duplex, and in the steps that connect the levels the style reaches its apotheosis. Granted that only fifty per cent of a regular staircase is used, since just one foot presses on each step, what does the architect do? Lop off the redundant half, of course. Leaving steps that alternate, right, left, right, left, etcetera. True, the residents have tried to impress their personalities upon this chamber by decorating the walls with posters, but in their absence, devoid of their possessions, these emphasize the emptiness. Nor are there any books on the shelves, save my war poems, and a book marked with a single yellow star. The ghetto journal of a Warsaw Jew. The diary was discovered after the war, his body never was. Actually, I did not bring the book along to read, rather as a reminder of an evil that cannot be exorcized. Nevertheless, flat out with colic I read it from cover to cover. What can I say? In class we talk of literature but this is not art. The writer chronicles everything as dispassionately as possible, a record for future historians, until in the end he can restrain himself no longer. 'Daughter of Germany!' he curses. 'Blessed is he who will seize your babes and smash them against the rock!'

Sweet dreams! I dream of flesh in torment and awaken to find my body in a rash. No stranger to hives, I blame my brain, never suspecting the true culprits. But instead of fading, the hives swell so that by mid-morning, my class in full swing, they are throbbing in sympathy with the soldiers in the trenches. Fighting the temptation to scratch I ask my enemy to read Rosenberg's 'Louse Hunting'. Blushing she begins.

> 'Nudes, stark and glistening,
> Yelling in lurid glee. Grinning faces
> And raging limbs
> Whirl over the floor on fire;
> For a shirt verminously busy
> Yon soldier tore from his throat
> With oaths
> Godhead might shrink at, but not the lice . . .'

And gets no further. Bursting into tears she cries. 'You mock me! You see the bites on my neck and you think I am dirty! But only here have I got them! There are bugs in my bed!'

'She means Franz,' says someone, referring to my only male student, likewise bitten.

'My dictionary tells me that a bug is a ghost, a bogeyman, a night prowler,' says another, 'so Franz could be defined as a bedbug.'

'But they are not the only ones who have been bitten,' I say, 'look at my arms.' Whereupon my enemy regards me with something like gratitude. 'You see,' I say, 'the poems are relevant to our condition after all.'

Tonight it is my turn to amuse the students. So I have arranged a visit to the Cambridge Arts Theatre. Since the play is Ionesco's *The Lesson*, which ends with the pedagogue stabbing his pupil and donning Nazi uniform, we have made attendance voluntary. In the event I am accompanied only by my erstwhile enemy, Franz, and my most attractive acolyte. Naturally I am curious to see how my charges will react to the drama. Franz and Monika fidget as the dead girl drops immodestly into a chair and her professor pulls on his swastika armband. On the other hand Inge is impressed.

'Such a play explains much about fascism,' she says, 'and about Germany.'

'Perhaps Germany as it was,' says Franz, 'but today things are different.'

'Nonsense,' says Inge, 'we remain a nation of *hausfrauen* who thrive on order. We didn't like the Jews so we make them disappear. Just like dust. We were frightened by the Baader-Meinhof gang so we killed them. Pouf! No more terrorism. We adore neatness. That is why Monika is horrified by her bedbugs. They leave marks. So she cannot forget them. She cannot sweep them under the carpet – is that what you say?'

'Suicide,' says Franz, 'they killed themselves.'

'That is what we are told,' says Inge, 'what you are pleased to believe.'

Monika looks at Franz.

'We must go,' he says, 'we are tired.'

'Not me,' says Inge, 'the play has given me an appetite.'

The Castle, an unexceptional pub on the road back to college. We request drinks and curries. The landlord motions us to a table. It is midweek and the pub is deserted save for a couple sitting in a darkened corner. The man is not in his right mind.

'Tell me, George,' he says to the landlord, 'now the season is a fortnight old what do you think of our esteemed football team?'

'My name is not George,' says the landlord.

'No spunk, that's their problem,' he says, 'not enough aggression.'

'They've only lost two games,' says the landlord.

'But how many more?' says the man.

'Listen, George, you know everyone in Cambridge. You tell the manager I've got some advice for him. A bastard I may be, pardon my French – father was killed in the war before he had time to do the honourable thing – but I'm related to lords, the highest in the land. Therefore the manager will listen to me. Did you hear about that Aussie coach who showed his team newsreels of Nazi war crimes before a big match? That got their blood up! Went straight out and thrashed the opposition. I've plenty of ideas as good as that. I'm counting on you, George. Tell the manager the bastard wants to see him.'

'Wash your mouth out,' shouts the landlord, 'I won't have bad language in this pub. Not when there's ladies present. If you won't behave you can clear off.'

But Inge is not embarrassed. 'That was a fine play we saw tonight,' she says, 'perhaps we could produce something like that in our composition class?'

'Good idea,' I say, 'but it will be difficult with so many people. You and Monika will never agree about anything. You'll argue over every word and nothing will get written.'

'You are right, of course,' says Inge.

'Maybe we could do something with a smaller group,' I say, 'you, me and one or two others.'

'But then those who are left out might become envious,' says Inge. 'They will accuse us of elitism.'

'Then we must arrange a cabaret for the last night,' I say. 'Everyone will be invited to help. I'll advertise for poets, singers, even stripteasers. Our contribution will be the play.'

Inge laughs. Her shoulders tremble. Not for the first time I observe the body beneath the shirt.

Two plates of curry stand in the serving-hatch growing cold. We watch them while the landlord sulks. Finally I deliver them myself. But before we can begin our meal the loony snatches Inge's plate and scurries to his table.

'You've taken our dinner,' he yells, 'we were here before you!' His companion looks miserable, but remains silent.

As if awaiting this opportunity the landlord reappears. 'You have gone too far,' he bellows, 'apologize to these people at once!'

The man is outraged. He puckers his lips as if about to blow a kiss. 'Sir,' he says, 'it is they who should apologize to us for stealing our food.'

The landlord's wrath descends upon the lunatic who flees for his life.

'I might be illegitimate,' he cries into the night, 'but I do not copulate with Germans.'

Now I am angry. But I am a hypocrite, the half-wit is a prophet.

Brushing my teeth in preparation for bed there is a knock on the door. Foaming at the mouth I admit Inge.

'This afternoon I purchased equipment to purge your bedbugs,' she says. 'I planned to tell you after the theatre but the events in the pub drove it from my mind.'

I rinse out the toothpaste. Inge meanwhile is crumbling a firelighter into a large metal fruit-bowl and mixing the fragments with charcoal chips. The result is ignited. Flames leap from the bowl like tongues ravenous for bedbugs.

'Now we must wait,' says Inge, 'until the charcoal becomes red hot.'

We sit looking at one another.

'You are married?' says Inge.

'Yes,' I say.

'I am not married, though I have a man in Germany,' she says. 'Here I am free, there I am a prisoner. You understand? Always we must do what he wants. Do you know the word 'eudemonism'? It means you act for another's happiness. It is your moral duty. That is always the role of women, don't you think? Your wife, does she work?'

'No,' I say.

'Why not?' says Inge.

'She was pregnant,' I say, 'but she lost the baby. She is going back to work soon.'

'Is she – how do you say? – in a depression?' asks Inge.

'She is over it now,' I say, 'we don't talk about it any more.'

We feel the heat from the glowing coals.

'Let us hope the bowl does not crack,' says Inge, 'it isn't mine, it comes from my room.'

As if casting a spell she pours yellow powder on to the embers. Asphyxiating fumes immediately fill the room.

'Sulphur,' she says. 'The gas it makes will kill all the bugs.' Coughing I lead her upstairs.

We stare into the underworld.

'Look,' says Inge, 'as I said.'

Sure enough, bugs are dropping lifelessly from crannies in the ceiling. Suddenly an unexpected twang! The bowl has split.

'Oh, no,' cries Inge.

Brilliant as the steps are in conception it is dangerous to descend them at speed, as Inge learns. She tumbles, hits the floor with a thump, and remains utterly inert. Spreadeagled, supine. There is no blood, but I do not know if this is a good or a bad sign. Her hand is limp. I feel for the pulse, but it is either stopped or I have my thumb in the wrong spot. Her heart. Situated, of all places, beneath her left breast. I place my hand upon the breast. It is warm certainly. But I can feel no heartbeat, though the nipple tantalizingly hardens. However, for all I know this may be a posthumous reflex action or even the beginnings of *rigor mortis*. I am no doctor. At a loss I rock forward upon my knees and part her lips with my tongue, intending to administer the kiss of life. But as I begin to blow into her mouth I feel Inge's right arm curl around my neck. And as she presses me closer I realize that my hand is still upon her breast.

Bugs continue to fall as Inge glides out of her pants. Possessed now, I turn out the lights so that Inge's naked body is illuminated only by the smouldering charcoal, a serpentine shape, splashed with red, an undulant stream of lava into which I fling myself.

'Take me,' hisses Inge, 'here, as I am, on the floor.'

While the madness lasts I pump my body into her, aware only of our sweat and the uncontrollable pleasure, dimly conscious of the mocking parody the dying embers cast upon the wall. Spent, prone upon Inge's salty body, I gasp for breath in the sulphurous air.

'Please,' whispers Inge, 'I am not finished.' She directs my hand down her belly to a damper place. Slowly my senses settle as I watch Inge's spectre writhe, and listen to her ecstatic groans, which dissolve as a deeper voice fills my ear:

> 'Soon like a demons' pantomime
> This plunge was raging.
> See the silhouettes agape,
> See the gibbering shadows
> Mix with the baffled arms on the wall.'

A man emerges from the shadows. He is dressed in khaki and puttees, but looks too delicate to be a soldier. 'Do you like my poem?' he says.

'Yes,' I say, 'you were a genius.'

'Tell that to the Germans,' he says.

I nod. I am. 'Do you hate them?' I ask.

'You cannot hate the dead,' he says, 'and you lose touch with the living.'

Inge, oblivious, cavorts on the end of my finger.

'I'm doing this for you,' I say.

He shrugs. 'Why bother with humbug when you've got bedbugs?' he says. 'Jews, Germans, we're all the same to them. They have cosmopolitan sympathies. We destroy one another and the bedbugs take revenge.'

'Not here,' I say, 'they're all dead.'

'So am I,' he says.

'Do you remember my grandmother?' I ask. 'Eva Zelinsky, she lived near you in Oxford Street.'

'What does she look like?' he asks.

'An old lady, white hair, in her eighties,' I say.

He smiles. 'Everything changes,' he says, 'except the dead.'

'Aaaaaaah!' cries Inge. She comes, he goes. There is quiet in the room. Inge is drowsy with delight. The charcoal has burned itself out.

'Come,' I say, 'let's go to bed.' During the night I have a vision of bedbugs in congress.

Throughout the day Inge wears a silk scarf to conceal the bites upon her neck. Likewise, when I telephone my wife, I hide the truth from her. Better keep quiet and skip the consequences. In two weeks Inge will be back in Germany with her jailer. At the moment, however, she is in my room again. We are awaiting another girl, selected to complete our playwriting team.

'When you took off your clothes,' says Inge, 'I saw something. That you are a Jew. Please, you must tell me. When you fucked me, was it for revenge?'

I shake my head. 'No,' I say, 'I did it because I wanted you. I forgot you were a German.'

'I am glad,' says Inge. 'You know, I have always admired the Jewish people. You have read Martin Buber?'

'Buber? Sure,' I say. 'I know my melancholy fate is to turn every *thou* into an *it*, every person into a thing. Last night you were a *thou*, this afternoon already you are an *it*, last night we had intercourse, a real spiritual dialogue, this afternoon we must write dialogue.'

Inge grins, 'And do you have any ideas?' she says.

'No,' I say, 'I am the producer. Ideas are not my responsibility. Do you?'

'Only simple ones,' she says, 'like a husband and wife, eating dinner, watching television, talking but not communicating. Just one twist, a girl will be the husband and you must play the wife.'

The other girl arrives and accepts the idea with enthusiasm. We work on the play through the evening and into the night. The other girl goes. Inge stays. Martin Buber? A *boobe-myseh*!

On the last Saturday I escort all the students to Bury St Edmunds. A coach has been hired and I sit up beside the driver holding a microphone. As we approach the town along the Newmarket Road I indicate, to the left, the barracks where Rosenberg trained, on the right, my house. The coach halts in the large square at the top of Angel Hill.

'Okay,' I say, 'I'll tell you what there is to see in Bury St Edmunds. Opposite are the walls of the abbey, behind are the ruins and a park. There is a cathedral. Go up Abbeygate Street and you'll come to the market. Fruit. Vegetables. Junk. Beyond the market is Moyses Hall. Built by a Jew in 1180. Unfortunately for him all the Jews were expelled from Bury in 1190. Now off you go. Back here at three o'clock.'

Gradually the others slip away until I am left with only Inge for company. It is a hot day, dusty with heat. The locals look white and sweaty, like creatures unused to the light. The women wear drab moth-proofed frocks that show off the freckles on their breasts; the men roll up their shirt-sleeves to reveal the tattoos upon their arms. It is a mystery, this abundance of sample-book tattooing, all of course applied by choice. By contrast Inge's spectacular sexuality stops people in their tracks: her black scarf, her red tee-shirt, clinging like a second skin, her denim shorts and – this I know – no underwear.

'I feel so good today,' says Inge, 'I should like a souvenir. Is there perhaps a booth where we can have our photograph taken together?'

'There's one in Woolworth's,' I say. A photograph! Thus far the affair has been vague, nothing to do with my real life, as insubstantial as a dream. It will be a simple trick to persuade myself that it never happened. But a photograph! Our faces fixed, cheek by cheek, our relationship projected into the foreseeable future. Proof snatched from the lethal fingers of time.

The booth is already occupied by three small boys. We can see their legs, and hear their excited giggling. Then as the first flash fades we hear, above their laughter, the screech of a creature in terror. Inge tears back the curtain and exposes the boys, including one who is dangling a kitten by its tail in front of the camera. The kitten flails about uselessly, tensing and squealing in horror at each flash, only to redouble its efforts in the lacuna.

'You monsters,' cries Inge, 'stop torturing that poor animal!'

The boys grin. The kitten swings. Faster and faster. Until the boy lets go. The kitten lands on Inge's shoulder. Seeking to steady itself it raises its paw and sinks its claw into her ear. Inge gently lifts the kitten so her ear is not torn although the lobe is pierced and bleeding profusely, staining her tee-shirt a deeper red. I give her my hand-kerchief to press against the wound.

'It looks worse than it is,' says Inge, 'it does not hurt.'

'Nevertheless, you must come back to our house,' I say, 'you must wash and change. You can't go around covered in blood.' Once again a curious accident has left me with no choice. Inge will meet my wife.

We surprise my wife sunbathing naked in the garden.

'Hello, love,' she says, 'I didn't know you were bringing somebody back with you.'

'Only one of my students,' I say, 'she's been wounded.'

My wife, wrapping a towel around herself, approaches Inge and leads her off to the bathroom. They reappear in identical cotton shirts, bargains from the market. A stranger might take them for sisters. I cook omelettes for lunch, with a few beans from my garden, and serve them on the lawn where my wife had been alone less than an hour before. I am astonished how relaxed we all are. Inge rattles off examples of her lover's male chauvinism. We all laugh. I feel no guilt, my wife feels no pain. She suspects nothing. She waves the flies from our food and throws breadcrumbs down for the sparrows.

'Are you enjoying the course?' she asks.

'Very much,' says Inge, 'especially our little playwriting group. Has Joshua told you about our play? Yes? Of course. You must come to our cabaret and see it performed.'

'I shall look forward to that,' says my wife. She removes the plates and returns with a bowl of peaches. They are sweet and juicy and attract many wasps. Our fingers become sticky.

'I am glad everything is going so well,' says my wife, 'without any problems.'

'Only the bedbugs,' I say, 'look what they've done to my arms.'

'Poor thing,' says my wife, 'can't you move into a different room?'

'No need,' I say, 'they've been exterminated.'

My wife smiles. What contentment! I realize now why I feel so untroubled; I do not really believe that I have made love to Inge. She is what she seems, just a visitor. My wife is my wife. We belong. Cambridge is a foreign city. To which I must return, however.

I kiss my wife. 'See you on Wednesday,' I say.

'What a nuisance,' says Inge as the coach passes our house, 'I have left my scarf behind.'

'Never mind,' I say, 'I'll pick it up on Wednesday. Besides, you can hardly see the bites now.'

On Tuesday we complete the play. In the evening the heatwave breaks with a tremendous storm. Knowing how much my wife dreads thunder I telephone her. She does not answer. Later, when the rain has stopped, Inge and I stroll to the Castle to toast our success. Afterwards we return to my room where Inge now sleeps as a matter of course. In the morning I telephone my wife again. No reply. Probably shopping. Lunch over, teaching being at an end, I drive home to collect her. There are three milk bottles on the doorstep, the first already sour. Its top is off, filling the stagnant air with a nauseous odour. Within is a different smell, naggingly familiar. I shout my wife's name. But there is no response. The house seems deserted. Bedrooms, bathroom, dining-room, all empty. On the table is Inge's black scarf, neatly folded, and a note:

Don't forget this, Love Rachel.
PS. Hope the bedbugs have stopped biting Inge.

Then in the kitchen I realize what the smell reminds me of. A butcher's shop. Naked, legs splayed, my wife sits up on the kitchen floor with the wooden handle of our carving knife protruding from her belly. Her back rests against the wall, her arms hang stiffly down, her eyes are open wide. The blood is dry. It flowed down from her wound, between her thighs, and formed puddles on the floor. The only sound is the buzzing of flies. They walk upon her breasts, mass around her vagina where the hair is matted with blood. This horror is too shocking to be true! It is a phantasmagoria produced by my conscience. Art, not life.

'Your face is very white,' says Inge, 'is everything all right?'
'I'm just nervous about this evening,' I say.
We have gathered all the props we require; cutlery, crockery, sauce bottles, and a starting pistol loaded with blanks. And while Monika – of all people! – strips down to her underwear in front of the directors of Literature & Linguistics Ltd, Inge and I exchange clothes. A suit and tie for her, a dress for me. 'This is Cambridge,' I think, 'this is my life. There is nothing else.'
We hear Franz sing his folk songs. Then applause. We are joined by the third member of the cast. We walk out to cheers and laughter.
'Your wife is in the audience?' asks Inge.
'I hope so,' I say, 'she is coming by train.'
The play begins.
Inge – my husband – is a bank clerk. I am a housewife. The other girl is a television set. Inge orders me to switch her on. We hear the news. I serve dinner to my husband and our two children who are invisible. An argument develops between us over the boy's long curls.
'You'll turn your son into a pansy with your ways of bringing him up,' yells Inge.
'They're always my children when there is something the matter,'

I shout. 'I don't think you really wanted them. I won't forget how you treated me when I was pregnant. You didn't even try to hide your disgust. But you're the one who's disgusting!'

What am I talking about? Why am I pretending to be my wife? Wife? I have no wife. How these silly words have confused me! What next? Oh, yes, I am supposed to take the gun from my handbag. I point the gun at Inge. Why? Because I hate her. But why? Because she seduced me? Because she murdered my wife? Wife? I can't even remember her name. With her shirt and tie and pencil moustache, Inge looks like a creature from pre-war Berlin. I hate her because she is German. A Nazi! I fire the gun. The blast fills my head.

'Daughter of Germany!' I scream. 'Daughter of Germany!'

I shoot at her until the gun is empty.

Genesis

How Los Angeles has changed since my last visit! Then the giant sloth and the mastodon roamed the length of Wilshire Boulevard, the great condor nested in skyscraper cliffs, and I sported with a hairy woman. Her desires were those of an ignorant animal, too carnivorous for your fastidious narrator. Still we rolled upon the slimy grass beside black pools of oil and tar, gross symbols of her cyclopic sexual organs. She was growing dangerously impatient with my pussy-footing when our liaison was permanently fractured by the interruption of a sabre-toothed tiger. My immediate response was to tear it apart with my bare hands, but then I remembered the rules: no trespassing into the jurisdiction of the Angel of Death. So I shed my ballast and floated to freedom, while my unfortunate mate sank slowly into the sticky tarpit as the tiger roared its disapproval. What did she matter? She was only a character in a primitive drama.

Now what do I find upon that sentimental spot? A museum. To be precise, the George C. Page Museum of the La Brea Discoveries. Imagine my surprise when, wandering curiously among the reconstructed remains of my former hosts, I see a glass tomb containing the skeleton of a woman. As I stare at those bones in their dark container, flesh suddenly begins to grow upon them and I am once again in the presence of my ancient seducer. Even after all this time her powerful body is unmistakable, as is her voracious face. See how her long black locks tumble over her breasts, teasingly parted to reveal her nipples. She sensed I was exceptional, and begged me to share my knowledge with her. But it was forbidden. Now, nine thousand years later, she has got me into trouble. My imagination has developed the ability to create, and I quake for my hubris. Lucifer was shot down in flames for less. Then the vision disappears, and I am left staring into the sockets of a skull. A label beside the exhibit calmly informs me that I have experienced the magic of a three-dimensional hologram. Poor La Brea! What a way to spend eternity: to be recreated every couple of minutes as a lifeless golem! What a demonstration, also, of the limitations of human ingenuity. Forever the ape of God.

*

I have flown out of the shadows into the substance of your world. Where I dwell we are free from the contagion of language, our feelings float through the empyrean like balloons in a comic book. We lack appetites. We spin the Garden of Eden out of dreams, while you have transformed it into Safeways. In supermarkets the frozen lamb lies with the shark, the naked daughters of Eve smile knowingly from the magazine racks, and the fruits of the earth are gathered together. Pomegranates, persimmons, pears, plums, melons, peaches, potatoes, tomatoes, avocados, mangoes, gooseberries, strawberries, grapes, grapefruit, artichokes, asparagus, oranges, apricots, nectarines, figs; not forgetting apples. Nor is the tree of knowledge unshaken. Beside the varied versions of Eve other newspapers peddle forbidden fruit; the birth of a monster in Arkansas, the truth about the crack-up of a certain star's third marriage, a famous mother's heartbreak over her drug-addicted son. Only yesterday the thrifty shoppers of America were informed by the *Globe* or the *Star* that a recent spate of flying saucers were piloted by angels on a mission from God. A dunderhead preacher from the Deep South gave the *Globe*'s correspondent scientific proof that the angels were the Messiah's advance guard. Meanwhile, the *Star* reported that a Wyoming woman and her ailing child had been kidnapped by the angelic crew of a flying saucer. Within the craft they were forced to witness the horrible vivisection of a calf, which had inexplicably meritorious results. The child, the despair of doctors, was restored to health. Only I am qualified to judge the accuracy of these rumours, for I did land upon earth in a flying saucer, as my friend – the writer – observed. Driving down Laurel Canyon one evening last October he saw a yellow light flash across the smoggy sky. Without excitement he announced to his wife, 'I've just seen a UFO,' and thought no more about it. His sighting was confirmed on the eleven o'clock news. Now he sits at his desk, overlooking the Pacific, inventing his fictions. Awaiting inspiration he watches a whale swim breathtakingly past. Let me tell you a secret: his inspiration is actually telepathic communication. From an angel; to wit, me.

You will be curious about certain matters. Above all, you will want to know: does He exist? Certainly. In fact, He is your *sine qua non*. Be warned, your doubts are His despair; what *chutzpa* to question the existence of your creator! What is Heaven like? Like nothing on earth. Do angels have wings? No. We are not subject to the laws of gravity (we are equally exempt from the laws of space and time, not to mention fiction). Actually, gravity is one of God's stylistic flourishes; He invented it as a metaphor for the consequences of the original sin. A constant reminder of your condition. Just think! Adam and Eve eat an apple – Man falls. Years later Isaac Newton is snoozing beneath an apple tree. Suddenly he is awakened by the falling fruit, and twigs gravity. Hey presto – a scientific explanation for your earthbound state. Grounded by the gravity of the grave. As a result I walk around Los Angeles (where else?) with heavy steps, for my shoes are filled with lead. Without those weighty soles I would float back to Heaven like a bubble of helium. To find such shoes was not as easy as you might imagine, for the feet of angels are minute. Eventually I tracked down a pair on First Street in Little Tokyo. 'Never stray far from the Oriental quarter if you want to find shoes that fit,' advised the sales assistant.

Shod in Chinese slippers I shuffle from the Museum into a trio of demons sent to chastise me. They look like death, their transparent black flesh revealing all their muscles and bones. Yet they pass unnoticed among the crowd in Hancock Park attending the annual Festival of Masks. They are disguised as musicians, playing melancholy folk tunes upon antique instruments. Their disquieting thoughts reach me upon harmonious waves.

Something for your information: the only difference between angels and devils is one of occupation; angels are the Almighty's sycophants, whereas devils are His secret service. Heaven is Utopia. Perfect because it is only theoretical; you know what your writers say, theories would be fine if only there weren't politicians to put them into practice. But Hell is material, sure enough; a place of exile, the exquisite conclusion of all your mass movements. In short, your political philosophies begin in Heaven and end in Hell. Among its tortured denizens are those who questioned the ethical foundations of Heaven; what right had it to tranquillity when its substantial counterpart, God's creation, was in agony? Several angels demanded that God do something about the suffering on earth, and were sent straight to Hell for their pains. My brother among them. Being one of God's favourites, I dared ask for clemency. WHY SUCH A SHEMOZZL OVER A FEW EARTHLINGS? AFTER ALL, THEY ARE MERELY FIGMENTS OF MY IMAGINATION. SUBSTANCE WITHOUT SPIRIT. Like creators everywhere, God felt that His critics misunderstood His intentions. He agreed that humanity's misfortunes were upsetting, but insisted that this was a deliberate effect

of His art. PERHAPS MY TALENT FOR VERISIMILI-
TUDE IS A LITTLE DISTURBING, BUT YOU MUST
REMEMBER THAT WHAT YOU SEE IS NOT REAL.
IT IS A FICTION. HEAVEN CAN BE DULL. THAT'S
WHY I CREATED THE WORLD. TO PROVIDE MY
SUBJECTS WITH AN INFINITE SOURCE OF EN-
TERTAINMENT. AND BELIEVE ME, WITHOUT
TSURIS THERE WOULD BE NO STORIES. Then God
offered me a deal. (Forgive the capitals, but I could hardly use an image
like the burning bush; these days no one – except the *Globe* – would
believe it.) Anyway – the deal. Freedom for my brother if I could spend
a year on earth without becoming involved in one of God's plots.
KEEP AWAY FROM WOMEN, cautioned God, RE-
MEMBER WHAT HAPPENED LAST TIME. He wanted to
test my objectivity.

It was all very well for God to warn me off women, but the unearthly
beauty of my shining face makes me irresistible to them. Of course their
carnal desires are of little interest to me, but I can't just tell them to
get lost; besides, without a woman I am dangerously vulnerable to
lecherous men. Therefore, the Festival of Masks is a godsend. At last,
among the masked, I can wander freely – unmasked, unmolested. I am
admired not for myself, but for what others take to be my brilliant
costume. Indeed, the Park is littered with abandoned selves. Even
innocent children are lining up to have their faces painted by men with
chalky visages, red noses, and black eyes. Oh, yes, everyone is anxious
to improve upon the appearance vouchsafed them by their Maker.
Obviously, deep in their minds is the idea of masked revel, an anonymous inconsequential bacchanalia, but I'll tell you what image comes
to me: the toyshop in *Coppelia*. I love the ballet. It is the only one of
your art forms that gives an inkling of what it is like to be divine. How
I rejoice, from the obscurity of my seat in the gods, to see the dancers
defy gravity. What a ballet-dancer I would make! My *entrechats* would
be the talk of Los Angeles.

As well as the decorated children there are men and women merry-
makers disguised by masks made of papier-mâché, feathers and plaster
of paris, as gargoyles, birds, horses and demons. Alchemy is at work.
The sun, turning coppery as Copernicus had predicted, is transmuting
the smog into fool's gold. Gradually the grass ceases to be green, as
darkness imprisons the prism, and eyes no longer dazzle the brain with

impressions of the carnival. Instead, noses – excited by hitherto unnoticed perfumes of hotdog, kebab, tortilla, coffee and marijuana – contact the stomach via the nervous system. As if with one mind the crowds begin to make for the portable dinettes that enclose them in a square. Manikins, masks and marionettes watch open-eyed as their former admirers are blinded to their charms by aroused appetites. Somehow the twilight makes everything more grotesque; the masks look like the disembodied faces that haunt a guilty conscience, while the marionettes hang from the scaffolding like a row of political prisoners.

Abandoned now, 'Masques du Ballet' is minded by a man whose melancholy eyes belie the grinning mouthpiece he sports. His lips resemble scarlet bananas. His teeth look like piano ivories. But his eyes are real, and for a moment I am sure that he can see right through me, that he knows what I am. He knows, all right – not that I am an angel, but that I am his wife's destiny. For years husband and wife have been trying to conceive: all medical remedies have been sampled, wonder rabbis have been consulted; they have made love dosed with pills, lubricated with ointments and ornamented with amulets. But again and again they are defeated by the man's helplessly low sperm count. Eventually, broken by his wife's frantic desire for a child, he has agreed to artificial insemination. The next problem – a donor. His wife refuses to countenance the unknown medical student, and demands the right to choose the baby's father for herself. She is a fussy woman and thus far no candidate has sufficed. Until she sees me. Her unspoken desires bombard me; better than Nijinsky, better than Nureyev, better even than Barishnikov!

'That's the man!'

But her cry is unnecessary. Her husband knows, hence those sad eyes. I know. Her mask twitches, as though her real face were ready to burst with excitement. Standing beside her husband she looks like a swan on stilts. I flee as fast as my feet will carry me.

It is the mating season. The orchard that clings to the slopes of my garden is in blossom. The air is thick with pollen. Branches are heavy with birds obediently reproducing the species; for example, this pair of hooded orioles. She lowers her back, her wings vibrate, while he lightly lands upon her rump. From the western windows of the house I rent high on Mystic Way I can see the golden crust of Laguna Beach, and the unformed waters of the Pacific Ocean. Just now the grey whales are returning from the warm lagoons of Baja California, the pregnant females leading the new-born pups to their home waters off Alaska. The path of their migration is exactly as it was nine thousand years ago, foreshortened only by the infrequent ice-age. They provide the one continuity with my previous visit; everything else has changed, except perhaps the flight pattern of pelicans. Being immortal, I have been spared these seasonal movements, for there are neither births nor deaths in Heaven. Nor are there mansions. We live like whales in the water, in ecological harmony with the clouds. But here, on earth, I must copy my facsimiles and acquire a roof for my head; thus my permanent status is disguised by my temporary residence. And how do I finance my splendid hacienda? Well, in the backyard is the aerodynamic masterpiece that ferried me through the hellish heat of the earth's atmosphere, erroneously identified by my neighbours as one of Buckminster Fuller's geodesic domes. I have converted the interior into an ultra-modern gymnasium, which I advertise as the Academy of Anti-Gravity. I have assumed the credentials and credibility of an orthopaedist and run weekly Gravity Guidance Workshops for which I charge outrageous fees.

At the commencement of each class my patients don their Gravity Inversion Boots (patented by me, in partnership with my Oriental shoe supplier) and climb the wooden bars, from which they hang upside down for the best part of an hour, during which I demonstrate an uncommon variety of postures designed to combat the compressive force of gravity on the human spine.

'Is this what you call alignment awareness education?' asks one of my gulls.

'I don't appease gravity, I piss upon it,' I thunder. 'You want Rolfing? Go to a Rolfer!'

'How do you intend to release my body's natural energy flow,' he whispers, 'without moving me towards verticality?'

I am merciless. I bend outward at the knees, I straighten, I bend, I straighten ... and continue upwards until my fingertips are almost at the apex of the A-frame which encloses the gym. Eyes filled with adoration, mouths agape, my batty pupils call me magus, though I joke that it is all done with magnets. Repenting my pride I explain that my spectacular abilities are based upon the springy strength of the syssarcosis in my legs, available to all with the proper exercise. Nevertheless, my leap is considered something of a phenomenon by aficionados of gossip. Soon my reputation spreads to balletomanes who arrive to see for themselves. And are astounded. After them come ballet-dancers anxious to acquire my secrets. Before long I am coaching several in private, while fending off the advances of both genders.

My most persistent suitor is Nancy, a statuesque woman some six feet tall. She towers above the other acolytes at my Wednesday night class, her flushed forehead glistening at the apogee of her hundredth plié. Proud and strong, she still joins the après-gymnastics line-up, patiently awaiting her turn for an attempt at seduction. Being well trained my students unconsciously form an even gradient from the shortest in the front to the tallest at the back. Thus Nancy is the lucky girl who gets me alone. She disguises self-loathing with aggression.

'I suppose you think I'm a freak,' she says. 'A giantess who wants to be a ballerina. Well, I'm sick of the conventional wisdom that says ballerinas have to be as fragile as fairies. For God's sake, dancers are tough, they've got the stamina of marathon runners. So why the pretence? Because of a few outmoded conventions dreamed up during some of the most autocratic régimes in history? You'll never see me tangled in the tulle of a tutu. My choreography is rugged, earthy, my feet are bare, my costume is a body stocking.' She hesitates. 'Sometimes I dance naked. Would you be interested in a *pas de deux*?'

I shake my head, which she bites off. 'So you're just like all the rest!' she yells. 'You want to screw sylphs. You've got no balls, you fucking Ariel!'

Her fit of vulgarity is followed by tears.

'Goddamn my sex!' she cries. 'All my adolescence I dreamed of being a ballerina. But my body had other ideas. It grew and grew. Who am I kidding with my kung fu? My fate is always to want what I cannot have: a career, children – you.' She laughs. 'The trouble with me is that I'm too big for my boots.' Self-pity signals defeat.

'Enough,' I say, 'it's time for zero gravity.'

Showered, powdered, my students stand at attention beside the Samadhi flotation tanks. The contraptions come from San Francisco. One of the company's sales representatives invited me for a 'be-with session' immediately after I had sampled the experience, hoping to catch me in an over-receptive frame of mind. When I ordered six, you could feel his faith in zero gravity suddenly ascend to the clouds. But it's true enough: a little while in one of these tanks and an average human is amenable to any suggestion.

Deprived of all senses, my pupils lie upon salt water with the tank lids closed upon them. Out they step hours later, blank pages ready to be rewritten for my angelic amusement. In my cramped laboratory I repeat God's universal experiment. Tod and Bob are lovers, so I persuade Bob to couple with Nancy while Tod watches in tears. I allow the charade to develop until Tod tries to strangle Bob with his leotard. With six students the permutations are endless. One week Nancy is involved in a lesbian relationship with Ilana, the next she is on her knees among the men. I invent lusts and gratifications, and wonder at the passions I unleash. Thanks to the hot water in the tanks the risk of unwanted pregnancies is close to nil, nor do the characters retain any recollections. They return home with but one memory: their love for me. Her senses still reeling, Nancy wants me to accompany her, 'to see how the other half lives'.

'Come and meet my husband, the failed writer,' she says.

Why on earth do I accept such an invitation? Am I experiencing previously unknown feelings such as guilt? Impossible! Guilt is as alien to angels as loneliness. Or is it curiosity, that damnable motive? Whatever the reason, I drive down to their place the following Friday.

Their apartment is a dilapidated beachfront duplex in the grubbiest section of Malibu. By the time I track it down, the sacrificed sun is already bleeding into the Pacific. A somewhat primitive image, you may think, but no sooner have I been admitted than Nancy lights two candles in honour of the Sabbath.

'*Shabbat shalom*,' she says. Then kisses me on the mouth. 'It makes a change not having to stoop,' she adds.

Her diminutive husband, Artie, approaches from the dismal shadows of his silent study. His melancholy eyes are unmistakable. 'Welcome,' he says.

Welcome! Only by imagining themselves in the prow of a schooner bound for the Orient could habitation in such a dump be tolerable. We slump into beanbags sipping Zinfandel. On the walls of the lounge are a variety of masks, the swan's head Nancy had worn on the day of the festival being perched menacingly above my seat.

'We have a proposition for you,' begins Artie. Is he really artful enough to persuade an angel into bed with his wife?

'Go on, you fool,' prompts Nancy, 'he's not a mind reader.'

'I want you to sleep with Nancy,' says Artie.

He explains about his sterility. The idiot, does he actually believe that he can snare me in his plot? But before I can dismiss the offer the earth shakes, as one of the local fault lines slips, dropping the swan's head upon my own.

'Me Leda,' laughs Nancy, 'you Zeus.'

My anger knows no bounds; it is greater than the weights in my shoes and I fly to the ceiling. Blinded by the mask I crash around the upper reaches of the room, while my hosts watch thunder-struck. But angels don't experience anger! The thought that I might be losing control returns me to terra firma.

'Now you know,' I say, 'I'm an angel.'

'Save that for the *National Enquirer*,' snaps Artie. Deep-set jealousy prevents him seeing anything but a pagan phallic performance; already he is attempting to divine the meaning of which my acrobatics are but a symbolic manifestation.

Nancy's interpretation is no less self-centred. 'Will I learn to levitate like that?' she asks.

'Certainly,' I reply. 'Next Wednesday we'll all hold hands and float through the roof.'

She goes through it soon enough, metaphorically speaking, when I reject Artie's request. She calls me a snob, says I think I'm too good for her; worse, she knows she is right. Sadly Artie invites me into his study for a man-to-man talk. His wife's passion has failed, as will his resignation. What do I know of compassion?

Believe it or not, Artie's study is papered with rejection slips. His bookshelves are filled with the volumes of his acclaimed contemporaries, only a small space in the bottom right-hand corner being reserved for the few magazines that have published his stories. Closer inspection of the walls reveals that strata are slowly being formed; printed rejections are the bed-rock, above those are the personal rebuffs – like the one from *Esquire* which reads, 'Dear Mr Wiseman, A special story, but not special enough' – and finally, providing a very sparse top layer, are the acceptances.

'You shouldn't take it all so personally,' I say.

He looks at me as if I were mad. 'So who else are they rejecting,' he cries, 'Mahatma Gandhi?'

'Adopt the detachment of the voyeur,' I advise.

'There's only one thing I want to adopt at the moment,' he replies, 'and that's your child.'

'No,' I say, 'it's out of the question. I cannot risk attachments.'

For some reason this animates Artie. 'What are you, emotionally retarded?' he shouts. 'At the age of ten I was a regular little monster, pulling the pigtails of girls in the school-yard and making them cry. Then I had a dream. I don't remember what it was about, but it changed me. As a result I lost my freedom of action. I guess I grew a conscience, or something. Where's yours, mister?'

I have no answer, nor do I like the expression on his face, so I look towards the window instead. Not twenty feet away is another building, which consists of four apartments. One of the windows is illuminated, and within a girl is pacing back and forth. She is wearing a red dress. But not for long. Her brassière is one of those that unhook at the front. She opens it like a book to show me her breasts. They have a curious effect upon me; my breathing is no longer relaxed, nor is my heartbeat regular. Needless to say, the girl has no interest in the condition of my respiratory system. Seeing her standing there, stark naked, nearly takes my feet off the ground for a second time. I have to concentrate upon faking my gravity.

'I see you've spotted our night club,' says Artie. His grin is sly. I laugh but I accept his invitation to stay for dinner.

Soon I am a regular Friday night guest. Naturally, neither Artie nor Nancy has an inkling of the real reason for my frequent visits; they assume our growing friendship is gradually lowering my resistance. But they are as wrong as those who believed the earth was flat so that if you sailed far enough you would drop off the edge. Without fail I find some excuse to spend time alone in Artie's study, which enables me to watch the girl prepare herself for the weekend. It is a game I do not always win. Sometimes I am frustrated by her avocado plant, the leaves of which cover her nakedness. Or she turns her face towards me, so that I must go on all fours for fear of discovery. On those occasions I emerge in an evil temper, and take it out upon Nancy the following Wednesday. To compensate for such disappointments I begin to keep a log of my successes; jotting down such remarks as 'Fine sight of her breasts as she lifted her hands to curl her hair'; or: 'Excellent view of pudenda as she administered vaginal deodorant.' But there are glorious instances when I can feast my eyes upon her entire anatomy, newly minted by the setting sun. Like some Ptolemaic astronomer she thinks herself the centre of the universe, inspecting her reflection in the mirror, but of course she is merely a moon held in weekly orbit by the gravity of my desire. Then I re-enter the dining-room in an elated state. Mistaking my motivation, Artie and Nancy exchange hopeful glances.

One Friday when I arrive at the apartment as usual only Nancy is home.

'Where's Artie?' I ask.

'Don't you read the newspapers?' Nancy replies. 'The Klan fire-bombed the Temple yesterday. He's on guard duty tonight.'

However, this selfless act does not prevent Nancy from trying to seduce me yet again. And to my horror I find that I am weakening, that I actually consider intercourse with no little pleasure. For in my imagination the woman squirming beneath is not Nancy but the girl whose body I have mapped in secret without ever seeing her face. She is the abstraction of sexual desire, of which Nancy is a material counterpart. I must have been lost in a daydream, for I am suddenly aware that Nancy has betrayed my jeans to gravity. Not only are they crumpled around my ankles, but my shirt is also unbuttoned to the waist. Nancy, likewise, is no longer dressed. She stares at me in wonder.

'You're not circumcised!' she exclaims. She is so taken aback to discover that I am not Jewish that she fails to notice an even more significant feature: a belly without a belly-button. Angels are immaculate, and knowing God we require no religion. A gnosticism Nancy is prepared to forgive when she spies my erection. But biblical knowing would be unforgivable. Briefly, if I copulated with Nancy she would be burned to a crisp. A price Nancy seems prepared to pay.

'Please, Nancy,' I say, 'I like Artie too much to do this to him, especially tonight. Besides, we're not in this for pleasure but to reproduce. Let me collect my sperm in a jar, and we'll impregnate you by hand.' Otherwise Artie would do better to run home with his fire-extinguisher. Nancy remains unconvinced until my penis decides the issue by ceasing its anti-gravitational antic. So I shuffle shackle-ankled into Artie's study to masturbate while Nancy curses my behind.

No sooner do I look at the window than the girl's image develops upon the glass. Off comes her dress, up goes my periscope. But instead of removing her underwear she executes a series of yoga exercises she didn't learn at the Academy of Anti-Gravity. My penis is in bud, but it will not open until she is fully exposed. Frustration causes me to groan out loud. At which Nancy bursts in, and seeing at last the true object of my appetites she cries out:

'That slut had an abortion less than three months ago!'

But I am too far gone to care, and groan even louder as she finally parts company with her brassière and steps out of her pants – to reveal yet another layer. But have no fear, she disposes of her sanitary towel as expertly as a stripper slips off her G-string. She is naked and I am lost. As my semen hits the bottom of an empty jar of artichoke hearts I know that I was mistaken about planetary motion. That girl is no moon. On the contrary, I am her satellite. I am subject to her comings and goings, not she to my desires. She pulls me towards her, at specific times, and now she has even drawn the semen from my body. Only one season has passed and already I am in danger. I turn to Nancy, frightened for my future. Incensed, she dips a poultry-baster in the pot labelled HEARTS OF GOLD and squeezes the liquid into her vagina.

'Ouch,' she hisses, 'it's hot!'

Nine months later my child is due, although Artie is naturally credited with its paternity. He actually wants me to attend the birth, but I refuse. What has it to do with me? Half-way through the proceedings I get a telephone call. It is Artie.

'Come quick,' he begs, 'Nancy's in trouble.'

I find her flat-out on a table in the labour room, an intravenous drip affixed to her wrist through which she is being fed glucose. In addition a bevy of attachments is strapped to her belly. She smiles at me.

'It's so silly,' she says, 'everything was going so well, then the labour stopped.'

'They got worried about the baby,' Artie explains.

The baby's heart is displayed on a foetal monitor; the figure jumps between 140 and 90. Each time it drops to 90 I will it back up again. Always it responds. Until, without warning, it dives to zero. And there it remains.

Artie doesn't. He rushes into the corridor, yelling. I cannot believe my helplessness. The obstetrician smiling demonstrates that the baby's apparent death was caused by a microphone sliding off Nancy's un-dulant abdomen. Shortly thereafter Nancy's wrist is penetrated by a second tube, through which pitocin is administered. Thus stimulated by the hormonal equivalent of inspiration her womb heaves, complet-ing its dilation and catapulting the baby's head into the vagina. Simultaneously the foetal monitor registers the severity of the contraction on a tongue of paper that unrolls from its intestines. Nancy, waving, is wheeled into the delivery room.

Eight days afterwards I am invited to my son's circumcision.

I have not been to the apartment for some time, thinking it tactful to keep my distance. Besides, I needed to prove to myself that I possessed the will-power to break away from the girl in the window – that I was still independent. Don't forget, the baby is Artie's dependant, not mine. And how happy it makes him! 'I've never seen Artie looking so pleased,' I tell Nancy.

'Yes,' she replies, 'he's beaten his creative block at last.'

'Because of the child?' I ask.

'Heavens no!' she says. 'He's been to a workshop. A potent brew. Creative writing and Jin Shin Do.'

'It helped?'

'You bet,' says Nancy. 'You should hear him explain how acupressure has opened up new territories of the imagination. No more typing for Artie, he taps his acupoints instead, and waits for the energy to flow. What a workshop! He sang the body electric. Also fucked his instructor on her yoga mat.'

Artie approaches, laughing. 'Nancy's jealous that I had better luck with my teacher than she had with you,' he says.

'Sweetheart,' snaps Nancy, 'you may have learned the language of the body and how to embody yourself in language, but words are about the limit of your body-building abilities.'

Artie winks, turning Nancy against me.

'It wouldn't do you any harm to read Artie's latest story,' she continues. 'The act of love – narrated by a penis. You see, Artie's been taught to empathize with his liberated organs.'

The door-bell chimes. Artie hurries to admit the rabbi.

'It'll serve you right if you identify with your son's penis tonight!' shouts Nancy.

There are no circumcisions in Heaven, so I am caught unawares by the intensity of the occasion. The baby is strapped into an Olympus Circumstraint by the *mohel*, whereupon his jaw trembles, his tongue flutters in his open mouth, and his face turns bright red. He howls in anticipation of the awful sacrifice, notwithstanding Artie's attempts to calm him with a pinkie dipped in kosher wine. I begin to feel somewhat queasy, as if the walls of the room were closing in upon me. I want to push them away, but my hands are bound. I scream. Someone pushes a finger in my mouth. A large face hangs above me. Where are his hands? Pain! Pain! A plastic cap is forced over the head of my penis. Snap go the surgical scissors. The rabbi concludes the ceremony with the traditional blessings, but they fall on deaf ears – for I have fainted.

'Unfasten his tie,' commands the *mohel*, 'take off his shoes!'

When I recover my senses I am lying with a bag of ice upon my forehead. None the less, it is my feet that are cold, *sans* shoes, *sans* socks.

'Give me air,' I mumble. I stumble barefoot into the Los Angeles night, a fallen angel. I stare at the stars in the heavens, an infinite distance away, and see the former Academy of Anti-Gravity graduate into darkness. I shake as Copernicus must have done when he confirmed his terrible suspicions.

Somewhere God will be laughing, as His minions communicate their report. I have breathed life into a sterile womb, and now I will have to pay with my own death. I weep for my fate. I weep for my brother. I weep for my son. But if I am doomed to become the shade of a shadow I can still turn Artie into a man of substance. He publishes a book. It becomes a best-seller. What's more, the critics love it. 'Artie Wiseman,' reports the *New York Review of Books*, 'writes like an angel.'

The Incredible Case of the Stack o' Wheats Murders

It was a red-letter day for Joshua Smolinsky, private eye. No kooks, cretins or clients had come to call. On the contrary, he was entertaining Sir Isaiah Berlin. They were sipping VSOP brandy and discussing famous terrorists. Bakunin, among others. 'Morally careless,' Sir Isaiah called him, 'intellectually irresponsible, a man who, in his love for humanity in the abstract, was prepared, like Robespierre, to wade through seas of blood; and thereby constitute a link in the tradition of cynical terrorism and unconcern for individual human beings, the practice of which is the main contribution of our own century, thus far, to political thought.'

Joshua Smolinsky nodded in agreement. 'You've reminded me of an incident that took place at the University of California about a year ago – not here in Los Angeles but up the coast at Santa Cruz.' He paused. 'Would you be interested?' he inquired.

'Please,' said Sir Isaiah, 'go ahead.'

'Ever heard of Les Krims?' asked Smolinsky.

Sir Isaiah shook his head.

'He's a photographer,' said Smolinsky. 'Takes some pretty weird shots. But don't get me wrong. He's not some pornographer. Actually, he's a Professor of Photography over at Buffalo. His name was across all the papers a few years ago. On account of four photographs included in a big exhibit at the Memphis Academy of Art. You see, some psycho objected to them and kidnapped the thirteen-year-old son of the curator to make his point. He offered the boy's life in exchange for the removal of the offending prints. Here's the joke: he didn't want his own son corrupted by the images. Of course the authorities complied. In fact, so many good citizens agreed with the lunatic's action that the

Mayor of Memphis was compelled to form a committee to decide if the photographs were obscene. As a matter of interest, they found them innocent.

'Anyway, back in 1972 an anonymous lecturer at Santa Cruz (the university won't name him for fear he'll be torn limb from limb) ordered a set of Les Krims's pictures for a course he was teaching on the aesthetics of photography. Ten prints, postcard size, arrived in a box. Each print depicted a naked woman sprawled in a provocative pose, in her bathroom, her bedroom, her kitchen, the front yard. All were bound, some were blindfolded, others gagged. All appeared to have been stabbed, for pools of blood spilled from their bodies. Suggestive imagery also implied that they had been raped. Beside each corpse was a pile of pancakes dripping with pats of melting butter, the Stack o' Wheats, the signature of the murderer. This gave the collection its title, *The Incredible Case of the Stack o' Wheats Murders*. On first viewing the photos were shocking, not least because they were extremely erotic. Did that make me a potential rapist or worse? Then my training took over, I began to seek clues. I soon surmised that the puddles were not blood but pints of chocolate syrup, and that the murderer was not me. Finally, I found the pictures amusing. As Les Krims no doubt intended. The complete portfolio of signed fourteen-by-seventeen-inch Kodalith prints on lightweight Strathmore paper (for which the box was a sampler) comes complete with eight ounces of Hershey's chocolate syrup and enough pancake mix to make one complete Stack o' Wheats.

'However, not everyone was amused. For years the box of photographs gathered dust uncatalogued in the Special Collections room of the library at Santa Cruz, until word was leaked by a sympathetic librarian to one of the many feminist organizations that had proliferated in the meantime. An angry article in the student newspaper accused the library of being soft on hard-core porn. Action was demanded. The photographs were stolen, then returned after lengthy negotiation.

'But this gesture was not sufficient for one woman. Her name was Deborah Spray. She hailed from Dallas, where she had been raped at knife-point aged fifteen. Her reaction was typical: not personal but universal. She seized moral superiority. Founded a group called Women Armed for Self-Protection. They taught themselves to use guns, with which they intended to execute rapists vigilante-style. Maybe she did, maybe she didn't. A bimbo like that could say or do anything. She even had another name. Nikki Craft. Well, she got wind of the Stack o' Wheats.

'She took a look. Next day Spray or Craft read in the *San Francisco Chronicle* about a young woman stabbed to death on Mount Tamalpais. The paper described her corpse as curled in the foetal position. Her blouse was drenched with blood. A dog licked her lifeless arm. Was there any connection between that crime and the box she had opened in Special Collections? Spray decided there was. Like a paranoid she dispensed with the distinction between art and life. Listen, Sir Isaiah. I'll confess that the pictures got me excited. But I'm not about to cut a girl to pieces. You've got to be crazy to start with. And if you're crazy enough you'll get all the stimulation you need from the news . . . Spray decided that the girls weren't really sleeping, that the chocolate syrup was really blood. Moved by moral urgency she swore vengeance upon the photographs in the name of all women everywhere.

'For two weeks she concentrated upon winning the trust of the women who staffed Special Collections. So successfully that my friend Rita Bottoms, department head, bent the rules to allow her to copy the photographs. Spray explained that she needed the copies for a class she was taking on Violence Against Women. Rita even helped Spray with her camera (a new one) and allowed her own shawl to be used as a backdrop. A week later Spray returned with a professional photographer, claiming that her first effort had been a failure. It was a Monday. Rita was off-duty, as Spray was aware. A librarian named Carol was in charge. She assisted Spray with her set, which consisted of a cup, an orange plate, knife, fork, spoon, a vase of roses and a flag which read: This is Violence Against Women. Carol returned to her office. The next thing she heard was hysterical laughter. Spray's. The photographer was shooting at top speed while Spray tore the Stack o' Wheats to shreds and poured chocolate syrup upon the remains. Carol opened her door. But was stopped in her tracks when Spray moved aggressively toward her. She was scared. Meanwhile the photographer continued his work, even snapping Carol although she was in obvious distress. Those photographs were subsequently published without Carol's permission, upsetting her so much that her health was affected. Spray was arrested and charged with conspiracy to destroy Library property. She called the charges fascist. She left behind the roses. And a note:

38

Dearest Rita, Carol, etcetera, My hope is that what has happened here today will not make your lives more complicated and that it will not be interpreted as anything personal to each of you. These roses are a symbol of my thanks for your helpfulness and understanding. With my love, Deborah Spray.

Concealed among the roses was a flask of chocolate syrup. Later Spray telephoned Rita Bottoms:

SPRAY: I just wanted to know if you had got my flowers and the note ... the roses and the note?

BOTTOMS: Yes.

SPRAY: I just wanted to let you know that there was something that I left in the vase by accident ... I wanted to let you know that it wasn't left there for any sort of symbolic meaning. It was a container of chocolate syrup that I brought in with the flowers ... I just forgot about it ... Listen, I know that Carol was pretty upset ... She said that her job had been placed in jeopardy and that she had a whole lot of concerns that she would like to talk about ... I wondered if there was anything specific that she had in mind ...?

BOTTOMS: What you did was an act of violence against her, wasn't it?

SPRAY: I'm really sorry that you felt you were manipulated ... I really don't like to manipulate people ...

BOTTOMS: Yes, but what you did was an act of violence against her.

SPRAY: I really didn't enjoy manipulating you ... It was just something I had to do.

'Give Spray credit, she'd planned the happening to the last detail. As she was destroying the Stack o' Wheats, her supporters were saturating the campus with fliers justifying her action. I quote:

Violent pornography is an expression of something profoundly real in male psychology. Violent pornography is the theory; rape is the practice. To expect women to tolerate the protection of this sadistic chic in their school library is unreasonable. Blacks would not tolerate the 'humorous' prints of Klan lynchings. Jews would not tolerate the satirical depiction of Jews in bakery ovens. To ask women to be good civil libertarians at a time when they are being mutilated, raped and murdered in massive numbers is to ask us to passively accept our own victimization. Today, 31 March 1980, I have destroyed the Stack o' Wheat prints by tearing them into pieces and pouring chocolate syrup over them. I destroy these women-hating prints in the name of all women who must live moment by moment with the awareness that they may become the

39

next statistic on some police file; for all women who must live their lives as if in a war zone, constantly on guard . . . I take sole responsibility for this artistic expression.

Singular art in the name of plurality! Sir Isaiah, I don't have to point out the logical flaws, exaggerations and misrepresentations to a gentleman of your intelligence, but I will say as a Jew I don't like the cheap image pilfered from the holocaust. Speak for yourself, Spray − I'll decide for myself what I will or will not tolerate. What egoism! What *chutzpa!*

'Lucky Spray. The university dropped the charges against her. In return Spray offered to reimburse the library for the damage. The bill amounted to $13. But that was not all she offered:

In addition, I offer to provide free of charge, a collection of all materials from the controversy about the prints and about my decision to destroy them in protest against violent pornography. This will help preserve what is now an essential part of the history of the University of California at Santa Cruz.

The library took the money. Spray also suggested an exhibit in the library foyer. No way: 'The Library retains the authority to arrange exhibitions and will not provide an additional forum for theatrical events.' In fact, Spray's collection is now in the Reserve Section of the library where it is on a twenty-four-hour watch.

'But the fun didn't stop there. Faculty members (who should have known better) sprang to her side, hundreds of students agitated on her behalf. A public forum was called to discuss the implications of the deed. During the course of that evening several professors stood up to thank Spray for bringing the issues into the open. Unconscious sexism was confessed. Braver souls spoke in favour of academic freedom. None of them recommended rape, mutilation or murder of women. Spray defended herself against charges of censorship. She recalled that, as a student in Dallas, she had denounced her school newspaper for refusing to print a poem with the word "uterus". I don't need to explain the association of "denounced" to you, Sir Isaiah. Spray's defence of disobedience was subsequently printed. A pretty piece. It looked like a redwood forest, so full was it with the letter "I"! "I confronted . . . I denounced . . . I ordered . . . I felt . . . I decided . . . I voice . . . I support . . . I hope . . . I have chosen." Thus were her moral approvals and disapprovals dealt out. Nor were her sacrifices forgotten.

I hope my commitment to this issue has been made clear. I have spent over $500 of my own money, and incurred significant debts, in making this action possible. One month of my life has been consumed in making the educational impact that was my intent from the beginning. My intent was not to repress or silence; quite the contrary. I have acted in the spirit of total creativity and have encouraged all to explore this realm within themselves.

'In recognition of such sacrifices Spray was nominated for the Chancellor's Undergraduate Award, given for "outstanding contribution to campus understanding of ethical principles", by David Cope, Provost of College V, Helene Moglen, Provost of Kresge, Gillian Greensite, Coordinator of Rape Prevention Education Program, Michael Rotkin, Lecturer in Community Studies, and Jack Churchill, her arresting officer. Good old Jack! He didn't want to arrest her in the first place. "I had no choice but to do my job and uphold the law. But I can still arrest people with love." Despite the fact that Spray's nomination contained over three hundred signatures, Chancellor Sinsheimer declined to give her the award. "I'm embarrassed that, as a student here, Deborah Spray hasn't learned more about the importance of intellectual and artistic freedom," he said. "And I'm disappointed that a number of our students and faculty haven't acquired a deeper appreciation of the meaning of freedom of expression."

'Rita Bottoms hit the roof. "I'm talking about some basic human issues, about the way human beings treat each other. So when I hear some of the faculty here refer to what she did as an act of civil disobedience, I want to puke. I am horrified she would be nominated for the Chancellor's prize." Spray was just as angry. She demanded an explanation from the Chancellor for his rejection. She threatened to disrupt the prize-giving with a demonstration. No idle threat.

'She graduated, of course. She's still in Santa Cruz, where you can be whatever you want, providing you have will enough. Actually, I saw her in Los Angeles last week. There she was on Century Park East holding up a placard which read, *HUSTLER* HAS BEEN TEARING UP WOMEN LONG ENOUGH, IT'S TIME FOR WOMEN TO START TEARING UP *HUSTLER*. Her group – the Preying Mantis Women's

Brigade – was after Larry Flynt. They ripped up his magazine and poured chocolate syrup upon the pieces.'

Joshua Smolinsky fell silent. He awaited Sir Isaiah Berlin's response.

Tzimtzum

Sometimes people act out of character. Observe my wife standing at the head of a group of demonstrators shouting, 'Death to the fascists!' The police, for their part, advance upon us in rows, protected from brick-bats by their perspex shields, and knock her to the ground. Immediately one of their number steps out of the ranks and drags Ruth away by the hair. I give chase but she is already behind the transparent wall and beyond my reach. Most of all I want to straighten her dress which has ridden up her thighs and uncovered her pants. She is spotted by a few Nazi youths, whom the police are escorting, and they wave their Union Jacks and yell, 'Give her to us! We know how to look after commie whores!' But the police are too engrossed in their own activities to hear, they have become voyeurs excited by their own violence. Those shields have conned them into believing that their actions will have no consequences. But they are wrong, I have the bruises to prove it.

The postman reads the address on the envelope, then delivers a note from my agent. It informs me that he is unable to find an American publisher for my latest book. This is a big disappointment.

'Any mail?' calls my wife from the bedroom.

'No,' I reply, burning the evidence in the grate.

'There's a peculiar smell in here,' says Ruth over breakfast.

'I burnt the toast,' I say.

Ruth has the morning off, since she has to go to court. In the witness box a policeman convincingly describes how my wife attacked him, compelling him to subdue and detain her. Ruth tells a different story. Nevertheless, she is found guilty and fined. The magistrate – no judge of character – adds that he is shocked to hear of a teacher behaving in such a manner, and hopes that her antics will not have a detrimental effect upon the pupils.

'At least we've made sure that there'll never be another National Front meeting held in our school,' says my wife during the victory celebration in the local pub.

The school is a large comprehensive in South-East London, with a great many West Indian and Asian pupils. Hence the outrage over the presence of the National Front. The forebodings are justified. That meeting, not Ruth's behaviour, is to blame for what happens next: the formation of anti-immigrant gangs led by white bullies.

Ruth is prejudiced to see the best in everyone, but even she can find no extenuating circumstances; so when black girls begin to weep inexplicably in the middle of lessons she asserts her power to maintain order. During the following staff-meeting she makes several proposals to improve the situation, involving discussion groups, outside speakers on race relations, and inter-racial parent-pupil-teacher sessions. But her recommendations are greeted with indifference by her fellow teachers and courteously killed by the headmaster. She hears the whispered comment, 'Ruth's being idealistic again.' This apathy depresses her even more than the disruption in her classes.

'No one was supportive,' she says. 'They're all prepared to sit and watch the school being torn in half. Am I being foolish wanting to do something? I would have given anything to have had one teacher stand up and say, "Ruth's right." Just one!'

Then there is a scandal. A Pakistani girl in the fifth-year claims she has been molested by a group of white sixth-formers. Naturally the culprits deny the charge. So the girl names a witness. The witness disappears. And suddenly the outbreak of racial bickering is over. Only one problem remains unresolved.

'The mother of the boy who ran away was in school today,' says Ruth. 'He's joined a religious commune in Sussex. She wants me to talk to him.'

The community is situated in a lordly estate on top of a hill. The gates give no clue as to its identity, but they are open. The grounds seem to be full of young students, all of whom wander around with self-absorbed smiles on their faces. The first notices we see are in the car park where spaces have been reserved for 'The Guardian' and 'The Chief'. We find a board which displays a plan of the domain, picking out buildings such as 'Dianetics', 'Testing', 'Success' and 'Head-quarters'. Beside it is a sign which informs us: 'All Visitors Must Register At Headquarters Immediately'. Which we endeavour to do. The front door of the Chief's mansion has two functions: it gives security, it asks questions. These are the questions: 'Do You Have A Good Personal Ethics Record?' and 'Are You Efficient And Can You Produce?' If the answers are in the affirmative you are invited within. We enter anyway.

At once a smiling attendant asks our business, and we tell him we are looking for a boy named Robin.

'What does he look like?' he asks.

'He is very beautiful,' replies Ruth.

'We are all beautiful here,' says the attendant. So Ruth shows him a photograph.

We are directed to a vegetable patch where Robin is busy cultivating orchids. Ruth is right. He looks like an angel. Bees buzz among the orchids, some even appear to be copulating with blooms that bear an uncanny resemblance to the female of their species.

'Will you come home with us?' Ruth asks Robin.

'No,' he says.

'Why not?' asks Ruth.

'You believe that the true purpose of education is to make people happy, don't you?' he says.

'Yes,' replies Ruth, but slowly.

'Are people happy?' he asks.

'No,' says Ruth.

'Therefore education is a failure,' he says.

'You can't make generalizations like that,' she says.

'Look around you,' he says. 'What do you see? Smiling faces everywhere. And what do you see at school? Only scowls. Why should I give up my smile for a scowl?'

It is an unanswerable question, so I ask another: 'What are you smiling at?'

'The world,' says Robin. 'Because it's mine. Because I am exactly where I want to be. Thinking can't get you there. Nothing can get you there, because you're there already. All you need is someone to say, "Hey, slow down! Everything's beautiful. You're where it's at." Look at these flowers. They're beautiful too, and they know it. They're so cool they don't even have to move to reproduce themselves. The bees do all the work for them. We aim to match their serenity.' With a dazzling smile Robin returns to his orchids. We return to our house in Greenwich.

The next Ruth hears of Robin is when she is summoned to court to give evidence on his behalf. He has been charged with exposure and indecent assault. Apparently it had been his habit to run through the park in the early evening and expose himself to women pedestrians taking the short cut from the railway station, no doubt in the hope that they would fling themselves upon his member and carry off his seed. This was tolerated until he grew bolder and began to grab between their legs as he trotted past. Eventually the police picked him up. No one could understand why he needed to pester women at all; with his looks he could have had any girl he desired. On the same day I travel to Cambridge to give a lecture to some German students on the subject of Isaac Bashevis Singer. My friend, who runs the summer school, greets me at the station. He accompanies me into the lecture theatre. I tell the students about *tzimtzum*, the cabbalistic doctrine which explains creativity as a synthesis of good and evil. I quote the example of Gimpel the Fool, who becomes a storyteller only after learning of his wife's infidelities. 'His new role is the only legitimate offspring of a marriage which produced six bastards,' I explain. When I have finished I ask if there are any questions. But there is only silence.

'It was all very new to them,' whispers my friend. We both sit looking at the downcast faces.

Suddenly a girl explodes. 'Will someone say something,' she cries, 'this silence is driving me mad!' Afterwards she approaches me to apologize.

'There is no need,' I say.

Her eyes fill with tears. I offer to buy her a drink. 'I know just how you felt,' I say. We are sitting on stools in front of the bar.

'No,' she says, 'you cannot understand. You are like the others, a Westerner. I am from the East. Before I came to Stuttgart I was in an East German prison for eighteen months. For seven weeks I was kept in solitary confinement. When they took me out I told them everything they wanted to know. They didn't even need to ask questions. I talked because I couldn't bear the silence.' She is trembling, and her eyes seek mine for reassurance.

'Why were you arrested?' I ask.

'Because of my boyfriend,' she says. 'He escaped to the West. When he was over he sent word for another girl to follow him – not me. Unfortunately she was a police informer. She gave them my name. It is hard to forgive such things. Now I have a different boyfriend. We live together. But my nightmares haven't left me. In my dreams my interrogator and my betrayer become confused. And it is true; fascism, communism – call them what you want – are matters of personality not politics. My faith in people has been destroyed. I have become a little paranoid. Some nights I am too frightened to sleep, so I stay awake and write poetry. My experiences have made me an artist. Now, thanks to you, I even have a name for my condition. I am suffering from *tzimtzum*.'

I also am no stranger to insomnia. Many nights I lie awake listening to the World Service of the BBC. At the moment my wife is sleeping through news of civil war, assassination and natural disaster. I recall the East German girl and imagine what dark productive hours we could share. Ruth's mouth opens slightly and her eyelids flicker as if something deep inside is rising to protest against my vision, but at the final moment it is smothered by sleep. She was home from the session before me.

'Did the lecture go well?' she asks.

'Fine,' I say, 'how about your court appearance?'

'Guess who was on the bench?' she says. 'That swine who fined me. I could see he thought I was to blame for Robin's misdemeanours. You could hear his mind ringing up the clichés: Sex Education, Permissive Society, Free Love.'

'So what happened?' I ask.

'He was bound over for psychiatric reports.'

In the morning I watch the postman walk by our house without pausing.

'Still nothing about America?' asks Ruth. She wants to show me sympathy, but doesn't dare. Success will bring us together, but failure is impossible to share. However, I do not want to blame our situation for what is really a flaw in my character. Let me give an example. During the Easter vacation Ruth invited a new teacher and his wife around for dinner; I'll call them Martin and Maria. We are introduced.

'Are you in the profession too?' asks Martin.

'No,' I say. Silence.

'What do you do?' asks Maria.

'I'm a writer,' I say.

Silence. Ruth, recognizing the symptoms, hurriedly offers drinks. Over dinner the conversation safely explores the subject of teaching. I do not say a word, because I have nothing to add. Nor do I join in when the discussion moves to the National Front.

'Believe me,' says Martin, 'they'll only be a force when they get a leader with real charisma.'

After they have gone Ruth turns on me. 'You might have made an effort,' she says. 'I want people to like you, not to think that you are a stuck-up bastard.'

'You know I'm shy,' I say.

'That's no excuse,' she says.

'Fascist,' I say. 'In a democracy all inhibitions must be respected.'

'You're the one with the fascist mentality,' she says. 'You guard your feelings as if they were state secrets.'

That night as usual my wife slept the sleep of the just.

We begin to see a lot of Martin and Maria. Martin is a music teacher. That is another problem; I am tone deaf.

'There's no such thing,' says Martin, 'you're just frightened to let go. Music is a great release mechanism. As far as I am concerned, a scream can be just as beautiful as Mozart. Come on, let's hear you scream.'

'Argh,' I say.

'You do have a problem,' says Martin, 'but it's nothing to do with music.'

Martin's dream is to start his own school. He has already opened an account at Barclay's in the school's name, which I won't mention.

'As I filled in those routine forms at the bank I could see my dream beginning to take shape,' he says. 'God knows, these aren't days for dreamers, but to me the whole concept has never seemed like a dream, more just the way it should be. Some pretty wonderful people are interested and want to be part of my scheme, including several professors. One day I plan to persuade Ruth to join us. She's wasted in the state system.'

Martin's ideas? He wants to build the school near Glastonbury, close to the source of England's collective unconscious. He believes, of course, that education should be directed at the heart not the head, that feeling is more important than thinking.

'In that case,' I say, 'how come you're so pleased to have the approval of the academics?'

'Why must you pick holes in everything?' asks Martin. 'If you're so suspicious why don't you sit in on one of my classes?'

At Ruth's insistence I attend Martin's elementary music class the following week, the first lesson of the new school year.

'I suppose you're all a bit nervous,' says Martin to the thirty odd thirteen-year-olds. 'Well, that's okay. Just don't try to hide your feelings. Music is all about expressing feelings. I'm also NER-VOUS! Now let's hear from you. What are you all?'

'NER-VOUS!' they shout.

'Very good,' says Martin, 'I think we've got the basis of a fine group here. Listen carefully, I want to explain what's going to happen. In the next three months we are all going to develop as human beings, we are going to communicate with one another by expressing our feelings through music. In that way I want you to tell me things you wouldn't dream of telling your parents. It's going to be a lot of hard work, but by the end of term I want us to be a group – not just an ordinary group – but a loving group.'

There are a few giggles at that, but I can see that most of the class is spellbound. Clearly, they have never heard such sentiments from a teacher before.

Martin decides to end the lesson with a sing-song. 'Something you all know,' he says, 'the National Anthem. I want everyone singing at the top of their voice. Miming will be regarded as an act of treachery.'

As Martin thumps out the tune on the piano the class roars its way through to the final 'God save the Queen', with the exception of an ungainly boy who makes fish-like gestures in a desperate attempt to conceal his crime. But Martin observes.

'Didn't you hear what I said?' he demands. 'What is the point of being here if you aren't prepared to join in? Everyone else is ready to take the risk of singing. Why should you be different?'

'I can't sing,' says the boy.

Martin smiles at me, acknowledging my presence for the first time. 'Yes, you can,' he says. 'There's no such thing as a bad voice, only a repressed one. Repressions stunt your growth. You do want to grow up, don't you?'

The boy nods. The class howls.

'I'm going to give you another chance,' says Martin, 'you sing, I'll play.'

The boy flounders hopelessly, so lost that he does not even notice when Martin begins to play the Marseillaise. However, his classmates do. They laugh joyously at their comrade's humiliation.

'Did you tune in to the feedback I was getting?' says Martin in the staff-room. 'Now perhaps you'll give some credit to my methods?'

'Don't you think you were a bit hard on that kid at the end?' I ask.

'I thought you'd single him out,' says Martin, 'a weedy mother's boy. Listen, when he's fucking girls at fifteen instead of blubbering into chicken soup he'll thank me for today.'

'But at the moment he hates you,' I say.

'Negative feelings are just as valid as positive ones,' he says. 'At least I've got him feeling.'

'Your school is going to be quite a place,' I say.

'You know, you could be a pretty good writer,' he says, 'if only you could free yourself of your obsession with structure. Loosen up a bit. Get a dialogue going with your unconscious. Then you'd be our ideal writer-in-residence.'

That evening, in bed, my wife asks me what I thought of Martin's class. 'The kids love him,' she adds. This statement makes me vindictive. I arouse Ruth, but refuse to have intercourse. She cries herself to sleep instead. Alone, I attempt to analyse Martin's 'dream', not according to standard symbols, but as an expression of his unconscious. If only I hadn't nodded off.

Glastonbury Tor can be interpreted in a variety of ways, with its single tower on top pointing directly to heaven. We are picnicking on its lower slopes, our food dispersed upon a blanket. Martin has artfully arranged a half-term trip for the sixth-form choir to Wells Cathedral, so he can look for a pocket of land on which to build his school. We have been invited along as fellow prospectors. I could not refuse, for some of Martin's enthusiasm has rubbed off on Ruth, and I sense that she has faith in him. This is disquieting. She talks about his 'presence', whereas I am described as 'remote'. It is a beautiful summer day. Martin, Maria and Ruth sit discussing the boundaries of education like three magicians, while I lackadaisically watch the swallows catch flies. Seeking greater stimulation I try to decipher a mirage that has formed where the ground begins to rise towards us. Gradually it resolves itself into a golden boy who is shimmering over the grass in our direction.

'We have raised the *genius loci*,' exclaims Martin. 'Welcome to where it's at.'

Robin smiles. 'Can't stop,' he says, 'I'm on the track of a rare orchid.' And returns to the heat haze whence he came.

'It's time we started moving,' says Martin. 'I want to go up the Tor and pick out a site for the school.'

'It's too hot,' complains Maria.

'And I get acrophobia,' I say.

'Can't sing, can't climb,' says Martin, 'you're a bit of a poor relation, aren't you?'

'Don't tease,' says Ruth, 'he really is terrified of heights. Please come,' she adds, 'I'll help you.'

'Go without me,' I say.

'Phobias are fascinating,' says Martin. 'I'm assisting a friend with his desensitization technique. What we'd do in your case is stand you on a table and relax you with music, so that you'd begin to associate high places with pleasurable sensations. Pity you think it's all mumbo-jumbo.'

'Oh, leave him,' says Ruth.

With Martin and Ruth gone it occurs to me that I have never been alone with Maria before. I look at her with a smile and suddenly become conscious of an unexpected set of associations; she chain smokes, she wears silver chains on both wrists and carries her watch on a chain around her neck.

'I know you're staring at me,' she says. 'Am I so interesting?' She snorts. 'Would it surprise you to learn that I see a shrink every week?'

'Why?' I inquire. 'You seem fine to me.'

'Oh, I function pretty well at surface level,' says Maria, 'but I'm right out of touch with my true self. I just can't seem to express what I'm really feeling. And of course Martin being so deep makes me feel even more inadequate. He's so patient, I only wish I could respond more. To tell you the truth, I'm afraid I'm frigid. That I don't display my emotions because I haven't got any.'

'So why are you crying?' I ask. 'I don't see any onions around.'

When Martin and Ruth return Maria's eyes are no longer puffy.

'Did you find somewhere?' she asks.

'Just the spot,' replies Martin.

'Plus we discovered Robin's orchids,' says Ruth.

'I've decided to adopt the orchid as a symbol for my school,' continues Martin. 'An orchid in bloom, roots and all. You know its name comes from the Greek word for testicles, because of the shape of its tubers. What a potent combination – beauty and virility! Our motto will be: "Power grows from the shaft of a phallus". In Greek, of course.' He laughs. Maria hugs her husband. Life isn't simple, but it isn't that complicated either.

Soon, however, life hands me a real complication. In the shape of an anonymous letter.

Thought you'd like to know. Your wife is making it with the music master.

'Anything in the post?' calls Ruth from the bathroom.

'Nothing interesting,' I answer. She no longer bothers to question me further.

'Why didn't you say there was something for me?' asks Ruth, having joined me at breakfast.

'Brown envelopes never contain anything important,' I reply.

'It's from Amnesty International,' says Ruth. 'Urgent action required in the case of Anatoly Shcharansky.'

The enclosure gives details of his trial, and quotes from his address to the court. 'I am happy that I have lived honestly and in peace with my conscience, and never lied even when I was threatened with death,' he said. 'I am happy to have helped people ...' His words vivify a character dormant in my memory. And Gimpel the Fool – equally consistent – repeats in my ear, 'I believed them, and I hope at least that did them some good ... What's the good of *not* believing? Today it's your wife you don't believe; tomorrow it's God Himself you won't take stock in.' This was Gimpel's foolishness; he believed what he was told. No sooner do I think of Shcharansky's trial in fictional terms than it becomes real. I see him in the courtroom talking to the wall. The audience remains silent until his sentence is pronounced. Then they break into spontaneous applause. 'It serves him right!' they yell. 'He should have got more!' He is called a weed that must be uprooted from Russia's sacred soil. And what was his crime? He told the truth. Most of us accept that the self must evolve to survive; we are chameleons, not leopards. When they tell us to sing, we sing. If it were possible I would weep. I did not help the boy in Martin's class, I cannot help Shcharansky. 'Anatoly,' I say, 'after the orchids have sickened and died they will ask you to make sense of the mess. Just hang on.'

Ruth is writing to President Brezhnev. But what can a letter do?

After school we play tennis with Martin and Maria. Mixed doubles. Martin is a superior player who demands the fullest concentration, but today my mind isn't on the match. I am watching Ruth for any signs that the letter might be true. Every time she serves I imagine that she is stretching to reach Martin, and rallies between them take on the air of an intimate conversation that excludes me. We are thrashed.

'What's the matter?' asks Ruth.

'Nothing,' I say. I no longer have it in my power to share my feelings with my wife. If I haven't already lost her, I soon will. I tell myself not to be so dramatic.

Unfortunately my subconscious refuses to accept the advice. My face turns green. So does Ruth's. We are walking through a coniferous forest, following the course of a fast-flowing river. Without warning, the motion of the water becomes perpendicular. The forest disappears. Our faces become white. We are on the edge of a precipice watching the river drop down the sheer side of a cliff. The effervescence makes the chasm seem bottomless. As it is winter the spray crystallizes on contact with the air, forming a great mound like a loaf of sugar. Ruth strolls towards the brink, nearer than I dare go. I have a sudden horror that she will vanish from my life. My heart freezes with fear.

'Ruth!' I cry. 'For God's sake come back here!' But she doesn't listen, and dissolves into the mist.

Then Robin appears. Since he has wings I ask him to hover above the waterfall and look for Ruth. Instead he pulls down his shorts, to reveal a bloody flower! Even insomniacs have nightmares.

Our decline continues.

'Did you have a good day?' asks my wife on her return from school.

'Not bad,' I say.

'What did you do?' she asks.

'Writing,' I reply. Whereupon she quits my study, and is usually not re-encountered until I find her in bed already asleep.

One day, however, I surprise her by responding in the affirmative.

'Yes?' she repeats.

'My agent phoned me an hour ago,' I say, 'he's sold the American rights for ten thousand dollars. We're rich!'

I make plans. I laugh. But Ruth is crying. Not for joy.

'We've got to part,' she says. I know some terrible revelation is on its way, and I feel my wife's pain in summoning up the courage to tell me.

'I'm in love with someone else,' she says at last.

'Martin?' I say. She nods. 'What do you mean by "in love"?' I ask. 'Have you slept with him?'

'As good as,' she says. 'We made love that afternoon at Glastonbury. It's funny, when I left you I had no intention of doing anything. I even said no when Martin first suggested it. I was very flattered, of course. A man like Martin saying he loved me. Then he said how much he needed me and I thought of you – how little you need me. That's when I said yes. Two words – "need" and "yes" – and it was done. Don't make any mistake, it was good. Martin told me not to feel any guilt, but he needn't have bothered. It was easy keeping up the pretence while you were being such a shit, but now you're suddenly nice again I can't pretend any longer.' She moans. It is extraordinary; her body is expressing my feelings.

'Do you want to leave me?' I ask.

'I don't know,' she says. 'I expected you to throw me out.'

'Do you still love me?' I ask.

'Of course,' she says.

'So what do you want to do?'

'I don't know.'

Silence. And in my solitude I dimly perceive the cruelty of the East German girl's tormentors. I also have been emptied of all sensations. Events have torn my stomach inside out. I also am ready to confess to anything. But confession will not alter the fact that my wife is in love with Martin. Slowly my tongue unrolls, until words pour from me in torrents. By mutual consent we make extreme efforts to save ourselves, ignoring any deeper damage for the sake of the moment. Indeed, it is impossible to do otherwise; future wretchedness cannot be put into words since it has no immediate expression. So our language is descriptive, our tense the present. We talk through the night and into the afternoon. School is abandoned. By evening we have reached a new *modus vivendi* that does not include Martin.

But such excommunication cannot be accomplished with a simple fiat. For one thing, Martin remains Ruth's colleague; for another, she still loves him. Consequently she insists upon telling him what has happened before he hears it on the nine o'clock news.

'Leave me alone,' she says. She dials his number. Secretly I pick up the extension. Martin answers simultaneously.

'Hello,' says Ruth, 'is Maria out?'

'Out cold, my amorous anima,' replies Martin. 'God, how I love you, Ruthie. I'd given up hoping to feel real love again. You've got grace, beauty, and such gut-level sensuality! You wanted me so much. Your body was like an instrument only I could play. Listen, I'm going to tell you a secret. When we climaxed together it was my first time in perfect harmony.' He pauses.

I can hear my wife breathing. Is she going to tell him? It is almost irrelevant now. I cannot burn Martin's words like an unwanted letter; on the contrary, they have been branded on my memory. Nor do I stop at words, images come unbidden. My enemy and my wife making love, in a hollow surrounded by trees, watched not by Robin but by me.

'I've told Jonathan everything,' says Ruth.

'Everything?'

'Yes.'

'Has he kicked you out?'

'No.'

'Are you leaving him?'

'No.'

'Do you love him?'

'Yes.'

'Do you love me?'

'Yes.'

'I see,' says Martin.

Is he holding back his tears? Ruth certainly isn't.

'If I can't be your lover, at least let me be your guide,' he says. 'Please don't think I'm being sceptical if I tell you a little story. It's about two friends who are going through an ugly experience. The root of their sickness is the one's insistence upon control of the other. Instead of two healthy people who appreciate each other for what they are, the man has tried to turn his wife into an appendage of himself. So that her psyche has become hopelessly entwined with him. I may not have taught you much, Ruthie, but I hope you'll always remember that a healthy selfness is a must for a sound love relationship.'

I feel nauseous. I replace the receiver as quietly as I can. But I cannot shut out the sight of their copulation. It reappears most frequently when we make love, and though I go through the motions I am not really participating. My wife is stimulating Martin, she is responding to his thrusts, she is wiping off his semen. I am merely watching from behind a tree.

Otherwise things are fine. Months pass. The government falls. Ruth sees Martin at school only when she has to. She goes off the pill in preparation for starting a baby. Then one day Martin walks up the garden path wearing an orchid in his buttonhole. It is the first time I have seen him since Glastonbury.

'Hello,' he says, 'I've come to ask for your votes.'

'Why?' I say.

'Didn't you know,' he says, 'I'm your National Front candidate for the general election?'

'You're joking,' says Ruth.

'Not at all,' says Martin. 'The National Front may be tainted with Nazi ideology but that's all old hat. It's today's radical movement. Labour is the party of reaction. Thirty years out of date. Why not open your minds to new ideas? No other party dares speak of the spiritual regeneration of the British people. Note the words, "spiritual regeneration". In the right hands the National Front could be the salvation of this country.'

'But it's fascist and racist,' protests Ruth.

'Don't be silly, Ruthie,' replies Martin, 'would I join an organization that was evil? Forget political prisoners. I'm here to liberate your minds. Mental terrorism, that's what I preach. Indian mysticism is all very well – you know how much respect I have for their religions and cults. But we British require something altogether more red-blooded. Like Robin, an angel with muscles. Or you, Ruthie. Your mixture of spirituality and earthy sexuality is just what we're looking for.'

'Please, Martin,' says Ruth, 'it's over.'

'Perhaps,' he says, 'but we both have a pretty clear picture of what happened. And why. The ballot is secret. Jonathan need never know if you put a cross by my name. Follow your heart on polling day, Ruthie. Vote for me.'

We are on the steps of the town hall when the election results are declared. Martin receives 600 votes. Ruth swears that hers is not among them. The victorious candidate is mobbed by his supporters, who do not include us. We have come as witnesses to failure, not success. We walk away.

Since it is a balmy spring night we decide to take a short cut through the woods. Ruth is reluctant, but I am persuasive. To frighten her I run ahead and hide behind a tree. Ruth chases me, then stops. There is a rustle of dead leaves and the bushes part. Ruth turns, expecting to see me, but faces instead her smiling attacker. Swift as an animal he pushes her to the ground and kneels on her left arm, simultaneously grabbing her other arm with his left hand. I watch, transfixed, as if in a dream. Ruth writhes about, calling my name. 'No, no, no!' she cries, words and sobs mingling. But she cannot prevent the angel-faced boy lifting her skirt with his free hand and pulling down her pants. Exposed, she lies still, sensing that any movement now is a provocation.

It is no use. He forces himself between her thighs and into her belly. Fighting for breath Ruth begs, 'Don't make me pregnant!' But her plea ends in gurgles and gasps. Faster and faster the figure pumps as if desperately trying to rise off the ground, until Ruth is activated by his passion and helplessly begins to heave in response. Out of control, her hands snatch for that final release which comes as a great shudder. Tears roll from her unblinking eyes.

I am Robin – out of character, as it were. 'You whore,' I say.

Somewhere over the Rainbow

The girl, furious, accused the man of a dirty crime. The man cringed.

'I was only looking for rainbows,' he said.

'In the middle of the night?' she replied.

To tell the truth, he had watched her undress. Her bedroom faced his studio and he had pretended that she was his model. Of course she was better than any model he could have booked, because her gestures were all completely natural. She was a figment of his imagination but also real, intangible but visible. At first she had slipped her dress over her head, without thinking, then she had paused, as if suspecting that she was being watched, but he had held his breath, and she had relaxed, and finally unhooked her brassière and stepped out of her pants. She was right, he had violated her body, but only in his mind. He had taken possession of her with his eyes, and the old adage was true: out of sight out of mind. Before him now, fully dressed, she was inviolable. He began to weep.

The girl was shocked, suddenly the roles were reversed, she was the aggressor and he was the victim. 'This is lunacy,' she thought. Then she remembered that lunacy was actually inspired by her new goddess, the moon. 'May I see your paintings?' she asked.

He led her to his studio, from which she could see straight into her bedroom. His paintings were terrible, misbegotten shapes in wild colours enclosed within heavy black outlines. She knew it was wrong to be judgmental, a throwback to the patriarchal system of academic criticism, and that she ought to be supportive – who knew what emotional risks he was taking in doing those paintings?

'I'd like one for my bedroom,' she said. 'How much do you want for the one with the tiger?'

'I don't know,' he replied, 'I've never sold a picture before.'

She wanted to be helpful. 'You should take them to the flea market next Sunday,' she said, 'I'm sure you'll sell lots.'

He began to laugh. 'Would you have said that to Rembrandt or Van

Gogh? Sell your paintings in the market. With all the other junk! These are works of art, worth more than a few pennies!'

'I think your paintings will be too expensive for me,' she said.

'It's a present,' he replied.

Then the girl saw that the man had not really lied when he said that he had been looking for rainbows, for there was a transparent rainbow pasted to his window through which the sunshine was radiating, splashing them with waves of multicoloured light. The man observed that the girl's face was an indefinable mixture of primary colours and explained that the reason he had come to her city was because of its reputation as the rainbow capital of the world.

'This area just seems to have a lot of people who are more in tune with the miraculous,' she agreed. 'There's an awful lot of heads and ex-heads who really get off on rainbows.'

'I want to let the colours wash away my straight lines,' the man said.

The girl liked this image, she thought it was very feminine.

'You've got factories that manufacture rainbows,' said the man, 'transparent ones for windows, five-foot long paper ones for walls. So why not a rainbow artist?' Then he spoilt it. 'My reward will be a pot of gold.'

'That's just the sort of materialistic remark you'd expect from a man,' the girl retorted. 'You'll never break out of your straitjacket if you keep up a language barrier between yourself and the ethereal.'

The man didn't know what to say. He looked so crestfallen that the girl kissed him on the cheek. 'Would you like a cup of tea?' he ventured.

'What sort?' she asked.

'Celestial Seasonings,' he replied.

'That'll do,' she said.

He poured the aromatic tea into brightly coloured cups from a pot shaped like a cloud with a rainbow for a handle. The steam made his eyes water. He seemed utterly helpless, without a vocabulary for the limbo land between the material and the ethereal. The girl took pity upon him.

'Would you like me to pose for you?' she asked.

He nodded.

She undressed. He didn't move. His eyes remained fixed upon her empty underwear, as if he couldn't quite grasp the implications of their vacancy. The girl understood that he was having problems adjusting to the reality she had created. She unbuttoned his shirt. But the erection her nudity had excited at a distance couldn't be repeated in close proximity. He tried to enter her limply, but even then his strength failed to materialize.

'My poor boy,' said the girl, 'forget about role-playing. Let me help you. My forearms are strong from milking goats.' As she pumped him the girl smiled, she had found the perfect man at last.

They exchanged gifts; she gave him a pair of rainbow-tinted spectacles moulded out of plastic, he gave her a painting. It consisted of eight hearts in two rows, each coloured differently – red, orange, yellow, green, blue, black, silver and rainbow. He had used water-colours and there were drips and smudges everywhere. Cissy was delighted, she named him her Rainbow Artist. He didn't dare tell her that he had copied it. They exchanged confidences; the man confessed that he was separated, Cissy confessed that she was pregnant. The man demonstrated how the affair had influenced his work, as thickening lines gradually encroached upon the polychromatic frenzy, until there was only black which marked the day his fiancée had finally returned his ring. She was a divorcée from Southern California with two half-breed brats (Cissy was shocked by such language) who refused to accept his artistic ambitions.

'Thanks to her,' the man said, 'I had two skins, one thin, the other thick; the latter being the pelt of a bear.' She had nagged him into a job at Disneyland. 'I felt emasculated,' said the man. His final humiliation had come when she had brought her kids to the Magic Kingdom and not recognized him beneath the ursine fur. 'Even when I took liberties with her that she should not have allowed a bare-face man,' he said. That's how he discovered she was a slut; when confronted with the evidence she called him a flip-flop, a flap-jack and a peeping tom, none of which he found flattering. Free once more, the future Rainbow Artist travelled north, hugging the Pacific coast until he reached the town of Oz, where he rented the studio that faced Cissy's bedroom. Another fifty miles would have brought him to Half Moon Bay, and a further thirty would have taken him all the way to San Francisco, where he could have remained as anonymous as he had been in Los Angeles.

Cissy's story was just as sad. Vampires, witches and ghosts strike fear in the heart of man because they have no reflections; men cannot stand beside them before a mirror and say, 'This is mine.' To be brief, without proof of possession, men sense they are possessed. Cissy presented no such problem; for years she had been nothing more than a reflection in men's eyes.

'I wanted them to think of me as sassy,' said Cissy, 'but I was an easy lay, that's all.' And so Cissy remained a sex object, punctured and penetrated by a hundred pins and pricks, until it came to the subject of her pregnancy. This was a consequence which threatened to become visible, and so destroy her image as an image. What was left for her? Overdose? Abortion? 'Anywhere else I would have sunk in waves of despair,' said Cissy, 'but Oz is a sheltered cove of high consciousness.' In fact, these words were a translation of her life and near-death; she washed down a box of tranquillizers with a bottle of vodka and with a head already swimming waded into the Pacific in search of oblivion; instead she was pulled·on board a sailing boat by the spiritual descendants of Atlantis. They cured her madness with hellebore, an ancient remedy, which is more commonly called bear's-foot. Consequently, Cissy and her Rainbow Artist could even exchange good-luck charms; a bear claw from him, some bear's-foot from her. And she knew more than ever that this was the man for her.

Once upon a time Luna would have been called a fortune-teller and forced to carry on her business within the context of a circus or a fun-fair, but in Oz she was able to set herself up as a clairvoyant analyst. If the future was of little interest she could also divine past lives, and make sense of the various reincarnations. Furthermore, she was adept at psychic diagnosis and soul reading; another sort of woman might have described herself as a good judge of character. But this is no comedy of manners; it is a story of masks and of hidden meaning, and of all possible masks language is the greatest.

The Rainbow Artist entered her office, which was tastefully decorated with the paraphernalia of her credo, and sat upon a comfortable rocking-chair. 'I have come to have my soul read,' he said. Ever since Cissy had told him what she wanted him to do, the Rainbow Artist had been apprehensive; most of all he was worried what his soul might reveal, that his soul might betray him to Luna as his tuberculosed lungs had betrayed him to a doctor years before. Nor was he sure that he wanted to know whether his soul was sick; such knowledge would make a sham of any subsequent good deeds, when he was bound helter-skelter for the shambles. Moreover, he did not think that Cissy would accept him if he were pronounced one of the damned.

Luna observed that her client was nervous, and sought to reassure him. 'You must not worry about a negative reading,' she said. 'With proper counselling we can restore the balance between your physical-etheric, mental and astral bodies which controls the health of your soul.'

She began to assemble certain objects upon her table, the mysterious appurtenances of her profession; no doubt the Rainbow Artist could have given a name to each of them, but their combination suggested the secrets of metaphysics.

'What do you do?' asked Luna.

'I paint rainbows,' replied the Rainbow Artist.

'You've certainly come to the right place,' said Luna. 'People here have been psychedelically baptized,' she continued, 'we're more than willing to tap into the vital energy that's reflected in rainbows.'

The Rainbow Artist recognized Cissy's sentiments, though Luna's language was considerably more scientific. She handed him a piece of paper with dots marked upon it.

'Do not think that this owes anything to the masculine science of geometry,' she said, 'this is geomancy.' As with many such controlled experiments, Luna's practice never varied. First she had her clients connect as many dots as they wished, then she poured sacred earth from a leather pouch into the palm of their hand and asked them to cast it upon a blank sheet of paper. She recorded the resulting patterns, comprehensible to her alone, with a Polaroid camera. They were like fingerprints, no two were ever the same. The Rainbow Artist watched, fascinated, as the photograph of his soul developed before his eyes.

He returned to Cissy with the good news that his soul had passed its medical. What had particularly impressed Luna was the realization that his masculine tendency toward worldly achievement had not obliterated his deeper feminine feeling for cosmic harmony. In short, the Rainbow Artist had not followed the example of ninety-nine per cent of her male clientele and closed all the dots; and this had coloured her divination of his earth-pattern, in which she had recognized an uncanny resemblance to the constellation of the Great Bear, Ursa Major. Her first reaction was one of disappointment, since it was supposed to exert a malign influence, but then she recalled the story of its creation and was mollified. How Callisto, a follower of chaste Diana the huntress, was seduced by Jupiter in her guise, much to the chagrin of Juno, who transformed poor Callisto into a bear. Here, surely, was the archetype of the suffering the Rainbow Artist had experienced at the hands of his fiancée in Disneyland: turned into a bear because he had the soul of an artist. In addition, the myth contained a mingling of the male and female elements which accorded exactly with her original intuition; how astute of Jupiter to realize that Callisto would only succumb to another woman's love!

With Luna's blessing the Rainbow Artist accompanied Cissy to her birth classes at the YWCA, mandatory for domestic nativities in the town of Oz. Their teacher was a midwife, heiress to the arcane wisdom of her calling, who preached natural childbirth and the perfidy of doctors. She called Cissy the Mother and the Rainbow Artist her Coach. She taught them deep breathing.

'Fill your lungs,' she ordered, 'then let it out slowly.'

They continued for a few minutes, until they took a cleansing breath.

'How did that feel?' she asked the Rainbow Artist.

'Weird,' he replied. 'I felt that my mind was floating away from my body.'

'That's good,' she said. She believed firmly in the ascendancy of the body over the mind, and taught that it was the Mother's job to follow the body's promptings throughout the birth. 'Your body will tell you what to do, for sure,' she said to Cissy. 'Learn to interpret its messages. Get in touch with your sphincter muscles.'

As the weeks progressed, the Rainbow Artist learned more and more about a woman's body, and learned how to help Cissy cope with the miracle of birth. Many times they went through a simulated labour together. But when the real thing began, they panicked; Cissy couldn't handle the unexpected severity of the pain, and the Rainbow Artist could think of no way to comfort her; all that they had learned to prepare them for the roles of Mother and Coach vanished into thin air.

When the midwife showed up at the Rainbow Artist's studio, Cissy was rolling in soiled clothes upon the couch, screaming for pethidine. This was not music to the midwife's ears. What was the problem? Not lack of love; she only delivered for couples who really loved one another. Inhibitions! They were fighting their bodies!

'Get undressed,' she ordered Cissy. 'Caress her,' she commanded the Rainbow Artist.

He began to stroke her hair.

'Touch her breasts!' cried the midwife. 'Watch me.' She stood behind Cissy and grabbed her breasts. 'See how nice they are,' she said.

She knew that a lot of women have a lot of things going with their breasts. For sure.

So the Rainbow Artist took up his position, and the midwife got Cissy to relax and ride her contractions. Thus they passed through the most agonizing period of labour, the transition, into that part when Cissy could take an active role and begin pushing. Crowning was followed by birth.

The Rainbow Artist regarded the new-born baby with amazement. It was lying upon Cissy's belly, still connected to her by the umbilical cord, gradually turning from blue to pink as its lungs filled with air and the oxygenated blood began to pump around its body. Although he was not the child's father he was happy beyond all expectation, tears fell freely from his eyes without his knowledge. Cissy yelped with delight; her perfect baby was howling on her belly, and her Rainbow Artist was clutching her by the hand.

'Did you feel it?' asked the midwife. 'The cosmic energy that flowed through you as you gave birth.'

Cissy had no words to describe her emotions, so she joyfully accepted the midwife's description. 'For sure,' she said.

With guidance from the midwife the Rainbow Artist cut the umbilical cord. Fifteen minutes later Cissy gave a final push and the placenta was expelled into the midwife's hands.

At that moment Luna arrived. She examined the placenta, like a priestess, and declared it free of blemishes. Again, the colours enthralled the Rainbow Artist: on one side it had a bluish sheen, which was criss-crossed with blood vessels, while the other side consisted of a dozen dull red lobules. Instead of wrapping it up and throwing it away, Luna and the midwife began to treat it as if it were something sacred. Indeed, Luna sliced thin wafers off the segmented side and pushed them between the lips of the assembly (with the exception of Baby). Luna considered the placenta to be divine, a miraculous source of life for the baby in the uterus; it was the female essence, the transubstantiation of all women into a single vital object. She placed the remainder in a reliquary. Finally, she noted down all the details required for an accurate horoscope; exact time of birth, etcetera.

It so happened that the week after Cissy's delivery was the winter solstice. What made it even more exciting for Luna was the fact that it was also a full moon.

Luna knew that in an earlier life she had been burnt at the stake as a witch; in trances she recalled the shame as the flames peeled off her clothes exposing her nakedness to the gawkers. A symbolic death! What better representation could there be for the fate of women? How many others had been killed in such a way since ancient times? Millions! Luna was ennobled by all these martyrs. They spoke with her voice. Victims of an unacknowledged civil war within society from which patriarchy had so far emerged triumphant. With what implications! For a start it meant that all folk tales were actually anti-feminist propaganda. Witches and stepmothers must be rehabilitated. Baba Yaga was really a persecuted herbal healer! Walt Disney was her arch-enemy. Although her particular *bête noire* was *Snow White*, she accepted *Sleeping Beauty* as the perfect model; a princess, poisoned by a jealous crone, who can only be revived by a man! 'Sweet Diana,' she prayed, 'give me revenge!'

After hours, as it were, Luna practised three kinds of magic: red, white, and black. Red was connected with cycles, menstruation, the seasons, fertility; its goddess was the moon, its expression was ritual. White magic was concerned with healing, black magic with cursing. Beneath the full moon, at the beginning of the longest night of the year, Luna performed red magic for a small group of witches, which included Cissy and the Rainbow Artist. They stood in a charmed circle at the summit of a hill. Luna compared the gross moon, unusually ruddy, with a placenta.

'In fact,' she said, 'each mother contains within herself a piece of the moon; just as the moon nourishes us, so the placenta nourishes our babies. We are all moon-children. Each month our Mother reminds us of our potential for fullness, but then shrinks in sorrow at our true condition. It is a reflection upon us. If all the people on earth, who are really the scattered fragments of the moon, could spiritually unite, the moon would remain forever full!'

The myth of Callisto was then re-enacted, with the Rainbow Artist playing Callisto transformed. He had felt uncomfortable in the bear-skin during rehearsals, until Luna had assured him that he would not be the anonymous buffoon he had been at Disneyland. As the moon rose higher, it shone with a cold light, which illuminated all too clearly the falling off there had been since classical times. In the distance the Pacific shimmered like a silver robe, while in the heavens the constellations watched the performance with indifference. Neverthe-less, Luna was exultant. At the ritual's end she proudly showed her fellow witches a flat cake she had baked which contained the dried and powdered remains of Cissy's placenta, taking literally the Greek meaning of the word. Slices were eaten by the assembled hosts, while the rest was buried beneath a puddle of moonlight to ensure a fruitful year.

The Rainbow Artist prospered. He opened a store called 'The End of the Rainbow', which specialized in artefacts connected with the colourful arc: he also sold teapots, cups, glasses, lamps, aprons, notepads and goodness knows what else, stamped with rainbows. From the rafters he hung shiny clouds from which dangled silken threads in a multitude of colours. On the floor he had countless arks, each stocked with all the animals of creation, including unicorns. Living brightly-coloured parrots flew around the store. The Rainbow Artist taught them to speak, but his vocabulary was not large, and they did not become great conversationalists. Cissy bought him a pair of green love-birds with blushing cheeks. They seemed content, though they preferred to remain in a corner perched side by side. In the centre of the store was a tall wrought-iron cage, topped by a dome, which contained the Rainbow Artist's most prized possession. A toucan. Its body was shiny and black, its eye was blue and its yellow beak was the shape of the rainbow. He regarded it with wonder, as if it were an emissary from a world of magical creatures. Occasionally the Rainbow Artist would display some of his own work on the walls; he painted rainbow-layered cakes and similar curiosities, as well as mystical landscapes which showed the moon connected to the earth by rainbows along which people travelled as if they were escalators.

One such hung in Luna's office. It had been a gift. She had said she liked it, so he had given it to her. She had seen into his soul and he could refuse her nothing. Luna was so pleased with the painting that she commissioned another. She had read that when Walt Disney had first created Steamboat Willie (the future Mickey Mouse) he had pencilled in a fight sequence between his hero and a tough sailor which left Steamboat Willie unconscious. Walt Disney had originally represented his state with a rainbow which flew from Willie's fuddled brain towards the horizon in a blur of colour. It was this scene which Luna wanted. The Rainbow Artist threw himself into his first commission with gusto. Times were good.

When he asked Cissy whether she was happy, she replied, 'Over the moon.'

Then Luna cast a spell.

Disneyland is another country. Admittance is controlled by blond boys and girls who sit in a row of booths like immigration officers at a border between states. Cissy, Baby and the Rainbow Artist passed through and entered the Magic Kingdom. They walked along Main Street. Here was the collective unconscious of America. Mechanical animals roared, mechanical savages waved spears, mechanical pirates shot one another; it all looked real, but no one was really hurt. There was no present in Disneyland, all was a dialogue between the past and the future; the present was the empty space through which a bullet passed between the gun and the target. Because the past had been conquered and rendered harmless, the future could be prophesied with confidence: it too would be a great age of mechanics, 'Autopia'.

Even the Rainbow Artist, who had smuggled unhappy memories past the officials at the gates, was won over by the spontaneous enthusiasm of Cissy and Baby. They clapped with delight at all the marvels the wizards behind the scenes had produced. Nor could he refuse Cissy's request to be photographed beside Mickey Mouse. As Cissy and Baby watched the Polaroid print develop, the Rainbow Artist walked up to Mickey Mouse and said, 'Bang! You're dead!'

The small gun in his hand repeated the phrase several times until Mickey got the message and fell down. The mask continued to smile, but the face beneath was distorted by pain.

'You lunatic!' shrieked Cissy. 'What have you done? What have you done?'

America

When I was little I thought *merica* was an English noun, always preceded by what my tutor called the indefinite article. Although I never heard it referred to in the plural I imagined that somewhere on Florianska Street there was a shop that specialized in selling a scintillating variety of *mericas*, which I visualized as enormous crystalline balls cunningly worked so that when struck by light they emitted countless golden rays. I was afraid of the dark and inclined to weep for my mother's eternal absence whenever she left me alone, but I never doubted the existence of the store. However, for such a sickly child the trip to Florianska Street (if made alone) was the equivalent of an expedition to the ends of the earth. Nevertheless, it remained my dream. I believed that my mother's brothers shared that dream, for it was they who uttered the magic word most frequently, but they never once offered to lead me to my childhood paradise. Instead, they looked upon it as their sacred duty to make me sturdy. Uncle Konrad would accompany me to the meadows beside the Vistula where we flew a kite.

'See how it wriggles in the sky,' Uncle Konrad cried, 'like bacteria under my microscope.'

Uncle Konrad was a biologist (killed during a cholera epidemic, coincidentally, by the bacteria my kite most resembled). Actually, as it was sucked further and further away, it reminded me more of the loathsome lozenges I was required to dissolve in my mouth every time I contracted a sore throat. Uncle Kazimir was an entomologist. He took me scrambling in the scrub that proliferated along the Route of the Eagles' Nests. Here he pointed out the manifold varieties of insect life. All of which disgusted me. Poor Uncle Kazimir. He died of fever in Ceylon, on a futile expedition. He travelled to the tropical isle with a group of fellow enthusiasts, only to be fatally discouraged by the local authorities, who explained that the beetles could not possibly be killed since they might be the reincarnation of someone's grandmother. Sure enough, Uncle Kazimir's name is now carried by a green beetle which inhabits the swampy region of the Danube delta. We preserved his collection of shiny bugs in glass cabinets like campaign medals. Only Uncle Lucian kept me entertained. He was a photographer. My greatest delight was to be smuggled into his studio and hidden behind the velvet drapes, where I pretended that I was snuggled beneath my mother's voluminous skirts, while he went about obtaining the portrait of a fine lady. Out of gratitude I determined to buy a *merica* for Uncle Lucian.

I lacked the courage for such an adventure and detested my cowardice. I fell sick. The family doctor said it was nerves and prescribed a tonic. My mother fretted; my father was unsympathetic. I got no stronger. One day the smelly Jewish girl who scrubbed our floors came to my room secretly with a silver amulet which she told me to put under my pillow. I held my nose as she knelt beside me to explain the curious symbols that were engraved upon it. She said that the bird, a comical creature the like of which I had never seen even at the zoological gardens in Warsaw, represented life.

'Why?' I asked.

'Don't argue,' she replied; 'the rabbi said so.'

But this did not satisfy me. I simply could not grasp how a bird could be the symbol of life, when the only birds I had seen at close quarters were destined to be plucked, cooked and devoured. Pullets, pigeons (delicious in squab pie), pheasants, partridges, songbirds, even a woodcock. It was true that Uncle Kazimir kept an owl in his study, but that creature dealt out death, not life. I never saw the owl without a dead mouse on the floor of its cage, its wicked beak clacking in anticipation. Then I remembered a word that I had heard at school many times, especially in Bible classes; this bird was a *sacrifice*! Like all the others it would die that I might live.

'Foolish boy,' clucked the Jewess, 'listen and don't ask questions. The first words mean "perfect healing". This word – *semerpad* – is a secret name for God. The next lines are a quotation from Genesis: "Joseph is a fruitful vine by a fountain; its branches run over the wall."'

'But my name is not Joseph,' I protested.

'My biggest boy is also not called Joseph,' she replied, 'but this charm still cured him of scarlet fever. Now he is as strong as an ox, *kayn aynhoreh*. Please God, you will soon be just as healthy.'

It was a good game, I decided, so I put the amulet beneath my pillow. I wanted to say something nice to the Jewess. 'You have a magnificent bosom,' I said, 'it is a crime to keep it so well concealed.'

Her reaction was frightening; she blushed like a schoolgirl and raised her hand as if to strike me. Yet the same words, spoken by Uncle Lucian to his clients, were always received with such gratitude.

When I recovered, the doctor claimed all the credit. But I knew whom to thank. To celebrate my return to the dining-table my mother ordered the cook to kill our fattest goose.

The dinner was a splendid occasion; not only were my parents and all my uncles and aunts present but also many friends and celebrated acquaintances. Because of the number of guests there were long delays between the abundant courses, so my mother permitted me to play in my hideout beneath the tablecloth. Consequently, I knew it was not clumsiness that caused the Jewess to spill soup upon my Aunt Amelia's shoulder but a squeeze on her calf from Uncle Lucian. I also knew whose shiny boot was rubbing against whose shapely ankle, though I could think of no reason for such activity. However, I had learned to keep my mouth shut; my indiscretion with the Jewess had taught me that adult behaviour was not as simple as it seemed. Now that I was better, the jaunts with my uncles were resumed, and once again I made up my mind to find a *merica* for my favourite. But this time I had a plan.

'I am going on a journey,' I told the Jewess, 'can your rabbi make a talisman to protect me?'

She laughed. 'So now you believe in them?' she said.

I recognized the question as rhetorical and did not answer. A few days afterwards the Jewess produced a second silver amulet.

'What does it say?' I asked.

'This one is more complicated,' said the Jewess. 'It begins with two four-letter names for God entwined, then it lists the angels who will watch over you – Gabriel, Michael, Badriel. The rest is written in code to deceive the evil eye.'

With that in my pocket I felt confident enough to walk unaccompanied through Planty Park.

It was early October and the park was alive with children collecting horse-chestnuts. Nannies sat upon the benches, casting benevolent glances in the direction of their charges, though they seemed more interested in the bold soldiers who sauntered past. Feeling carefree I also stopped to gather the newly fallen chestnuts, even then touched by the transience of their beauty. And with that thought came a glimmer of comprehension for Uncle Lucian's professional passion, and I could guess why so many women came to see him.

In a secluded corner of the park, when the town hall was already in sight, a young lout suddenly appeared. I called upon my guardian angels to protect me, whereupon a passing dove emptied its bowels upon the ruffian's head. And so I came safely into Rynek Główny, the Market Square. Fashionable women swirling parasols to deflect the heat of the autumn sun strolled through the Sukiennice, admiring the silks and laces on display, while their maids bartered with the peasants who had come in from the country to sell their produce. Since winter was inevitably approaching, many carts were full of firewood. 'Ready for delivery!' promised the drivers, as they prodded their old nags into life. Among all this bustle I recognized a familiar figure. His head was concealed beneath the black cloth of his camera, but Ignacy Krieger was unmistakable. There he stood like the man behind a Punch and Judy show, but he was the audience and the whole world was his stage.

'Hello, young man!' he shouted. 'What are you doing so far from home?'

'Shopping,' I replied grandly.

'Look what I have just purchased,' he said proudly as he gestured towards his glowing mahogany camera with its gleaming brass lens, 'a brand new Thornton Pickard, all the way from England. Just what I need for my street scenes. I'm afraid that your uncle is going to be very jealous.' Ignacy Krieger was one of Uncle Lucian's greatest rivals. 'Now that you are such a man-about-town,' he continued, 'you must visit my studio.'

Ignacy Krieger's famous studio! His obnoxious son Nathan, one of my classmates, never tired of boasting about his father's glorious studio with its ingenious gadgets. I was determined to strike a blow for my uncle. 'Not today,' I said, 'I am going to find a *merica* for Uncle Lucian.'

The sun illuminated Florianska Street, gilding the pedestrians and burnishing the shops. In the dazzling light the contents of each window looked like booty in a treasure chest. I saw diamonds, emeralds, rubies, silver cups, golden chains; I saw glossy furs, patent leather boots and a host of wonderful trinkets – but I saw no sign of a *merica*. At the end of the street I had to hold back my tears of disappointment. But I refused to give up the search: I knew that my uncle's main supplier, Fotografia Polska, was situated not far away on Krupnicza Street. Perhaps they would be able to help. The shop was full of familiar objects: bellows, lenses, tripods, cameras, all the paraphernalia Uncle Lucian adored. There were several glass discs, some concave, others convex, which slightly resembled what I had in mind. I approached the counter.

'What do you want, sonny?' said the supercilious salesman (I would report his lack of courtesy to Uncle Lucian, I thought).

I looked him straight in the eye. 'I want a *merica*,' I said.

'So do we all,' he said, 'so do we all.'

'I want a *merica*,' I repeated.

'Do you know what America is?' he asked.

I was angry, but I told him.

'You fool,' he guffawed, 'America is a country on the other side of the world.'

Utterly humiliated, my dream shattered, I left Fotografia Polska. Blinded with tears I began to run along Krupnicza Street, until the sun went down and the only light came from the gas lamps. My imagination tried to frighten me with wild possibilities, but I no longer believed in it. Even so, I did not dare walk back through Planty Park after dark; there may not have been any witches or goblins, but I was pretty sure there were bandits and kidnappers. Who could help me now? Only Gabriel, Badriel and Michael. Thanks to them I remembered that Awit Szubert, another of Uncle Lucian's rivals, had a studio at No. 7 Krupnicza Street. The door was not locked, so I ran up the stairs (carpeted, he was a successful man) and entered the studio just as the magnesium let rip. A small girl in a nightshirt was reclining on a settee opposite the camera; something about her pose made my hands tingle.

'Good heavens!' exclaimed Awit Szubert. 'What are you doing here?'

Yet again I wept.

'Play for a while, my pet,' said Awit Szubert, 'I must take this little gentleman home.'

My mother was shocked by my unorthodox arrival in a cab. Awit Szubert explained the circumstances.

'My poor boy,' cried my mother, 'weren't you afraid?'

'No,' I said, 'I was protected.' I showed her my amulet, with its Hebrew inscriptions and prominent Star of David.

'Where did you get this?' my mother demanded. She looked annoyed.

It was too much for me, after the day's disappointment. 'From Hannah the Jewess,' I wailed.

Then, with marvellous dexterity, Uncle Lucian (who seemed remarkably uncomfortable) saved the situation by jumbling the letters of AMERICA to form an ungrammatical English anagram that was also his autobiography, 'I CAMERA'. Even Awit Szubert laughed.

Years later I remember that afternoon with perfect clarity. Why not? America turned out to be my future also. Oh, yes, I found America in the end. Look at me now in a pisspot of the sleazy side of Hollywood Boulevard, my floor littered with empty Kodak film containers. My shutters are always closed. I have no desire to see the filthy posters nor read the flickering neon promises that lick the skies every night; instead I linger over the eloquent images that are windows on my past. This is the photograph Ignacy Krieger took that day in Rynek Główny, the cabs forever awaiting their fashionable passengers, who still promenade while their servants haggle, even though all the firewood has long since been burnt to ashes; and there in the foreground stands a lovely boy (myself) embarked upon his great adventure. This is my father taken by Awit Szubert (he hated his brothers-in-law, especially Uncle Lucian), his jacket buttoned to the throat in the manner of the time, parting to reveal a gold collar-stud, not a wrinkle on his fleshy face, his moustache finely pointed, his mutton-chop whiskers beautifully trimmed, his receding hair neatly combed (he did not live long enough to go bald), and such hope in his eyes. Ah – my beautiful mother! See how she clings to the polished oak banisters at the bottom of our great staircase, as if she would otherwise float away, her feet hidden by the wooden gryphon which now guards some other boy as he sleeps above. I recall how hard Awit Szubert (why not Uncle Lucian?) worked to make her smile, but all she could give him was a sorrowful gaze out of melancholy eyes (what was on her mind?). Her hair is parted in the middle and piled high upon the crown of her head. She wears rings and bracelets and holds a rose. The rest of her body is concealed by her dark constricting dress. I try to recapture the scent of the perfume she wore that day but it is a hopeless task. Here are some spectacular landscapes Awit Szubert took on our expedition to the Tatra Mountains. And this – which I dare not look at too frequently. A nude study, by Uncle Lucian, of Hannah. I am still grateful for the way she tried to comfort me after Awit Szubert had brought me home, and my mother had put me to bed. She came quietly into my room. What was she doing in the house at that hour?

'You are not the only person America has made a fool of,' she said. 'The biggest fool of all was Christopher Columbus. He thought it was India or Japan. Do you know he had a Jewish interpreter with him? Luis de Torres. Well, Louie goes up to the Red Indians and starts talking to them in Hebrew. He thinks he's in the East, you see? What a *schlemiel*! But at least he found gold in the *goldeneh medina*. Unlike my husband. Now there's a real *shmendrick* for you. A fool's paradise, that's all the *goldeneh medina* is to him. He can't even save enough to send for me. So how can he expect me to resist a *shmoozer* like your Uncle Lucian?' She pinched my cheek. 'You're a naughty boy, too,' she said. 'All that talk of bosoms. When you're bigger you'll be a real Casanova. The world will be at your feet.'

She should see me now.

I do not wish to speak ill of the Jews after all they have been through (Hannah included), but there is no doubt that they are responsible for my lamentable condition. By *they* I mean the Jewish moguls who control Hollywood. Perhaps they will remember me as the young man (young, alas, no longer) who used to deliver stills of the latest productions to their opulent offices. At that time I worked for one of the top production photographers in Hollywood. Since then we have all passed a good deal of water, as Mr Goldwyn put it. And I would be famous now, if not for *them*.

I had accumulated a wonderful collection of photographs of all the biggest stars which I was planning to publish. It would have made my name. But my agent got a phone call from a shyster lawyer warning him that I had infringed every copyright rule in the book. He dropped me like a hot potato. Next thing I knew my house had been burgled and all my negatives had vanished.

Why such persecution? Because of one night of madness with Errol Flynn, that's why! I met him at a big party up in Laurel Canyon. Errol's ribs were still sore from his notorious fight with John Huston, so he was boozing rather than whoring. He needed to be somewhere else so I offered to give him a ride (he was in no condition to drive). He tossed me the keys to his car. 'Take mine,' he said. We ended up in an unspeakable dive off Sunset Strip frequented by low life, actors, and gossip columnists, where we joined some of his German cronies.

Consider my position. I had come all the way to Los Angeles from

Poland only to discover that the City of Angels was not populated with the likes of Gabriel, Michael and Badriel, but with puffed-up Jewish pedlars whose cousins I could have seen any day of the week on Szeroka Street. Only now I was taking orders from *them*! Is it any wonder I cheered when Errol jumped on a table and did an impersonation of Adolf Hitler (in my opinion he was a much better actor than people said)?

'*Daloy gramotniye!*' I yelled, echoing the old war-cry of the Black Hundreds (coined for them by the Tsarist secret police for use during pogroms). Unfortunately, I forgot that most of the producers were Poles and that some of them were literate enough to know that the literates I wanted to do away with were Jews. The incident made the papers, pictures and all. Check the photo library of the *Los Angeles Times* if you don't believe me.

When it was too late we went back to my place. I lived in a modest house on Holly Drive, connected to the road by a steep flight of steps cut into the canyon wall. Errol staggered up them, miraculously keeping his balance, while hanging on to bottles of vodka and wine and a pot of caviare (which he had taken from a cache in his car). We drank, we ate, we told obscene stories (only Errol's were true). Soon the Germans were snoring. I felt wonderful. For a whole evening I had forgotten my lowly station in life; once more I was as bold as that boy who had gone in search of America. Drink had turned me into a sentimental fool. I showed Errol the photograph of my mother. 'A beautiful woman,' he agreed.

Then I gave him Hannah. She was three-quarters towards the camera, so that although her breasts and body hair were fully exposed, there seemed to be some reluctance in their display. She was bending slightly, allowing her full breasts to hang, so emphasizing their naked-ness. The sepia tone, the angle which revealed her shape so well, all gave this image of Hannah a three-dimensional effect which was not lost on Errol Flynn. He unbuttoned his flies and took out his famous instrument. 'This lady is about to be accorded a unique privilege,' he said. Whereupon he began to flick his penis lightly with the photo-graph. You must understand that the *cartes de visite* produced by Uncle Lucian and his contemporaries were not the flimsy things you get at drugstores nowadays but proper pieces of card. So Errol did not have any trouble producing an erection, nor in maintaining it. Poor Hannah took a beating that night. Luckily Errol Flynn's semen overshot her and landed upon my carpet. He left me to wipe it up, the animal. Next day I was on the blacklist.

Some job I found! Every night I tramp around the restaurants on Hollywood and Sunset with a camera supplied by my employer (not the Leica I demanded). 'Heil Hitler,' I say to the fat Jewish customers who are dining with their gaudy wives or cheap mistresses. (They hear, 'Smile mister.') How I despise them! So greasy is their hair that drops of oil collect on the tips like obscene ornaments. Oh, where are my mother's antimacassars? The women make a mockery of her discreet elegance with their vulgar display of valuable jewellery. Of course they are delighted to have their picture taken, their eyes send messages to mine ('Make me beautiful'), while their diamonds contact the light meter that turns the lens of my camera into a rhinestone monocle. And so I press the button and the shutter opens, letting in an image that will leave its contaminating stain upon my memory (among many others). I hand them my company's card. 'When will the print be ready?' they ask. 'Tomorrow,' I say.

But the night continues. Some restaurants are large enough to contain dance-halls. It is here that I meet my nemesis (again and again). High above my head a large ball spins suspended from the ceiling; covered with hundreds of tiny mirrors it sends scintillas of silver light cascading down through the smoke. Everyone longs for the brief feel of the spotlight. Except me. For the shaft misses my face and stabs me through the heart. My America! Why? Why?

Why did I ever leave Poland? When Uncle Lucian gave me my first camera on my fifteenth birthday I had no inkling that it would be the last birthday I was to spend in the company of my family. Indeed, my joy knew no bounds when my father informed me that I would be able to use my camera on Awit Szubert's next expedition to the Tatras. Awit Szubert had made an annual pilgrimage to the Tatra Mountains from the time dry bromide plates were first available in Poland a quarter of a century before. Now, to mark his twenty-fifth visit, he had invited all his fellow photographers and their families to accompany him. It needed a whole carriage on the Cracow to Zakopane train to accommodate us all.

The journey was exceedingly slow, due to the excessive number of curves and steep inclines the engine had to climb, but we didn't care as we gorged ourselves upon the contents of our delicious hampers. At last the train gathered speed as it steamed through the valley towards

76

Nowy Targ, the final station before Zakopane itself. After Nowy Targ the train began the ascent up the long gradient into Zakopane. As we traversed the terraced fields, the highlanders (still unselfconscious) in embroidered shirts, white felt trousers, broad belts and black hats, downed their tools to cheer, while their wives and children waved from the lofts of their wooden chalets, a spectacle which greatly excited Ignacy Krieger (who was planning the series on the traditional costumes of Poland which was to win him a gold medal at the Vienna exposition). In those days the mountains were pretty wild; the hidden valleys were well stocked with game, including wolves, bears and boars, and in the caves – so it was rumoured – were bands of brigands. Naturally, I pressed my face to the window in the hope of catching sight of the one or the other (without success).

At our destination the Mayor himself opened our carriage door and greeted Awit Szubert as if he were King of the Tatras. A pretty girl almost swooned when he kissed her on the cheek as she handed him a posy of wild flowers. A brass band struck up a melody of local tunes. The town was exuberant, and slightly pompous, for the people believed what foolish anthropologists had told them: that the Tatras were the birthplace of Polish civilization, and the cradle of a new independent Poland.

'Bah,' said Uncle Lucian.

Whenever I look at Awit Szubert's photographs memories of those first exhilarating days in the mountains come flooding back. There are six figures picked out against the snow in his study of Zawrat Mountain; I am closest to the camera; beside me is my father; ahead of us are Uncle Lucian, Ignacy Krieger, Nathan Krieger and our guide Jan (who claimed to have been a bandit in his youth). We didn't realize it at the time but we were carefully positioned to lead the viewer's eye towards the centre of the composition. A few minutes later my father and Uncle Lucian, who never liked one another, began to argue (maybe Uncle Lucian was upset because my father had commissioned Awit Szubert to take the family portraits).

'Please,' insisted Jan, 'you must never raise your voices in the mountains. The danger of avalanches is very great.'

My favourite excursion was to Morskie Oko, the Eye of the Sea. Legend had it that this beautiful lake was connected by underground tunnel to the sea some fifteen hundred metres below (but I didn't credit legend). Overladen with lunch packs and photographic equipment, we scrambled over the last rocky outcrops and gratefully flung ourselves down the shingle to its shores. Here we basked. As the sun rose higher in the sky the lake changed colour from blue to brilliant green, until it did indeed resemble a giant lens.

'Photography is no longer merely nature's pencil,' said Awit Szubert as he assembled his camera upon its tripod; 'now with the help of an accurate lens and light-sensitive plates I am able to reconstruct photographic images according to the rules of pictorial composition. I have become an artist.'

So saying, he shooed us out of sight so that we did not disturb the serene atmosphere with our lack of divinity. There are no boats on Morskie Oko in his photograph. But immediately afterwards the glassy calm of the lake was shattered by the launching of a dozen small dinghies. I found room on board with the Kriegers, while my father was left with only Uncle Lucian for company. We drifted around, overawed by the surrounding circle of mountains, until our reveries were scattered by an outbreak of hostilities between my father and my mother's brother. Although it was mainly commotion, odd words were carried across the lake to our boat. 'He is old enough ... He must be told ... Never ... I am his father.' Of course it was impossible to be sure who was saying what.

'Christopher,' said my father, 'what do you think of your Uncle Lucian?'

'I love him,' I replied.

'And me?' he asked.

'You are my father,' I said.

He continued his preparations without another word, nothing was going to spoil his big day. He had been looking forward to the hunt from the moment we arrived at Zakopane (it had long been his ambition to shoot a wild boar and hang its head over the fireplace in his smoking-room). But, as it turned out, it was a lucky day for boars. At first everything went according to plan. We slipped quietly into the forest below the Black Pond (where Awit Szubert was busy with another of his studies), searching the snow for footprints, watching the saplings and bushes for any slight movement that might betray the presence of a wild animal. Promising areas having been selected, the hunt began in earnest.

'Each of you has a horn,' said our guide. 'You must blow upon it as soon as you spot a boar. In no circumstance shoot until we are all accounted for. I want no accidents.'

Soon we were scattered in all parts of the forest. What occurred next is confused in my mind, and I am grateful that there are no photographs to settle the matter. It appeared that there were two figures in the distance gesticulating wildly; or perhaps one was waving his arms frantically, while the other was pointing a gun at him. Certainly we heard what sounded like shots, but they could have been the prelude to the louder crack that brought the snow toppling off the mountain peak. The image disintegrated. The air was filled with a million ice crystals, as though all the dots that combine to make up a photograph had exploded. Blinded and deafened, we were no longer witnesses. Thereafter, when we regrouped in a clearing, we deduced that the two figures must have been my father and Uncle Lucian. This was finally confirmed when Uncle Lucian was seen staggering towards us. Unfortunately my father was never seen again. What had happened?

'A terrible accident,' was all we could get from Uncle Lucian.

So that was the story we told my mother: that my father had been buried alive in a sudden avalanche. At least we were spared the funeral.

To tell you the truth, my father's permanent absence made little difference to his former household (of which I was now the head). However, the realization of my new status seemed to come as a shock to all concerned. My mother appeared more than usually preoccupied. (Surely she was not still mourning for my father?) As for Uncle Lucian, his moods were inexplicable and his behaviour incomprehensible. Time after time I would enter a room and find him deep in some intense conversation with my mother, only for him to draw away as soon as he saw me coming. I took to opening doors quietly in the hope of overhearing snatches of their dialogue, but all I caught were meaningless phrases. However, I was able to identify several instances of an 'either . . . or' construction associated with threats. And once (I swear) I heard my mother utter the word 'Blackmail'. After many weeks the disharmony subsided and was replaced by a duet, the key word of which seemed to be 'America'. Nevertheless, my mother did not recover her previous cheerful disposition.

On account of Uncle Lucian's strange behaviour since the accident, my visits to his studio had become more and more infrequent, until I stopped going there completely. But I resolved to make one more call, to confront Uncle Lucian man-to-man, if only for my mother's sake. His studio door was never locked during working hours (in the hope,

I suppose, that a customer turned away by Awit Szubert or Ignacy Krieger might find their way to his establishment), which was to my advantage as I wished to catch him unawares. Since he was busy with a client I slipped behind the velvet drapes where my childish counterpart had hidden so many times before. Fool that I was, I couldn't resist a peep. Standing on a pedestal where my uncle had placed her, Hannah completed the movement until she was facing the camera.

She was naked. I was astounded. I did not believe that women ever allowed men to see them in such a condition. And yet here I was, opposite Hannah, able to examine all her most secret parts.

'You must promise never to show that photograph to anyone,' she said.

Uncle Lucian laughed. He put his hand between her legs.

'Not today,' she said, 'I am fertile.'

'Very well,' said Uncle Lucian, 'kneel.'

Hannah knelt. She unbuttoned Uncle Lucian's trousers. He gasped. Hannah couldn't speak, her mouth was full. My own hands began to tingle, as they had at Awit Szubert's studio, and I imagined that Hannah's lips were pressed to my penis. Then imagination became reality as my hands forced Hannah's head against me, harder, harder ('Harder! Harder!' echoed Uncle Lucian), until my pants were oozing. Hannah quivered, as if with disgust, then wiped her mouth.

'What will become of him?' she asked.

'Christopher?' said Uncle Lucian.

'Our son,' replied Hannah.

'He is to start a new life,' said Uncle Lucian, 'in America.'

A new life indeed! And now it is nearly over. I am an old man, too decrepit to attract a woman. Hence my weekly visit to Mrs Klopstock's brothel (which has moved out to Santa Monica). You know all there is to know about me, so perhaps you would care to accompany me here too?

'I have a new girl for you tonight,' says Mrs Klopstock. 'You will find her in the "New Deal" room.'

Mrs Klopstock likes me, she thinks we have similar backgrounds; at any rate, we have aged together. The whore wears a wrap that she has not bothered to button, so that I can glimpse her nakedness beneath. Her body is not bad. Her face is also acceptable, though it shows the beginnings of a beard.

'I am Erica,' she says.

As I fuck her I make a pun (to myself, of course): 'This is my life in an Erica.' Perhaps I will leave her my beautiful photographs, to decorate her room.

Svoboda

'If you insist upon lying to me,' says my interrogator, 'perhaps you will have more respect for a rabbi.' He lights a cigar. 'Pure Havana,' he says, 'from our brothers in Cuba.' The tip of the butt, glowing through the smoke, reminds me of the day this all began.

The sun smouldered in a smoggy sky. They were having a script conference in Heaven. Perhaps my guardian angel was trying to set up my next assignment; as usual his idea was a bummer. An improbable beginning connected to an unlikely ending by outrageous coincidences. It was kicked out, leaving me unemployed. Dropped flaming from celestial heights, the pages drifted into Los Angeles on a bank of cloud, then sank with the sun. The afternoon was in ashes. Time to welcome Johnny Walker. After a few drinks the pigments of a man appeared upon the opaquely glazed surface of my office door. The colourful splashes refused to resolve themselves into a recognizable outline, even when the door opened. A gloomy hombre entered. Tears were flowing down his face.

'Damn the pollution,' he said, 'my eyes are full of grit.' Suddenly my visitor looked familiar.

'Feldman!' I exclaimed.

'Hello, Smolinsky,' he said.

'What brings you here?' I asked.

'Miriam,' he replied. 'She's disappeared. You're my last chance, Joshua. Find her, please.'

He was agitated. He tried to remove his contact lenses but was all thumbs, and one fell to the floor. We crawled about looking for it, like the poet who sought the moon in a pond. An easier job than tracking Miriam, last heard of in Czechoslovakia. Diplomatic inquiries had revealed nothing.

'Providence led me here,' said Feldman. 'I was walking aimlessly, hope gone, when a gust of wind smacked me in the face. Blinded with dirt I stumbled into a doorway. Blinking I saw the words, "Joshua Smolinsky, Private Investigator". I came right up. What do you say?'

I rose. Beneath my foot something crunched. What did I say? 'Sorry.'

Miriam was Feldman's crazy wife. Years ago we all used to go around together. Feldman and Miriam were both in the movie business. You've probably heard Miriam on the sound-track of a dozen weepies, playing onomatopoeic tunes on her violin. When Feldman first met her she was running with a crowd even loonier than herself. Their big ambition was to dump enough LSD into the reservoirs around LA to blow all our minds. Feldman – who was working on the script of a religious epic at the time – won her over with his spirituality. Thereafter Miriam turned her attention to the deeper recesses of the psyche. She got the notion that Hollywood was the manifestation of an overmind – taking the phrase 'dream factory' literally – into which the whole world could be plugged via the movies, television and video. So Feldman fixed her a job as his assistant, but all she got were rewrites of rewrites. Her own scripts never got near the ear of Morpheus. On the rebound she left Feldman and went underground, from where she bombarded him with anarchist manifestos. 'I do not want to be I,' she wrote, 'I want to be We.' Originality was not her strong point. I traced her to a hippie hacienda in Baja California. Feldman persuaded me to give him its location. There was a dreadful scene; nevertheless, they were reunited. Neither thanked me. After the Yom Kippur War, Miriam became a Zionist. Eventually she went to live alone on a kibbutz in the Negev Desert – to find herself. Last April she wrote Feldman a letter telling him that she was visiting Czechoslovakia to participate in the Prague spring music festival. A fortnight later he received a postcard from Prague. Since then, not a word.

'You've got to face it, Feldman,' I said, 'you've lost her.'

'All I want to know is that she's okay,' he said. 'That's not too much to ask, is it, Joshua?'

'Exactly what you said before,' I answered. 'Miriam hasn't spoken to me since.'

'This time it will be different,' he replied. 'If it's over, it's over.' He fumbled myopically for a chair. His cracked contact lens looked daggers at my conscience.

'You win,' I said, 'I'll go to Prague.'

'I cannot issue you with a visa,' the consular official said, 'because you no longer resemble the photograph in your passport.'

'What do you suggest I do?' I asked.

'Remove the beard,' replied the barbarous swine. But I stood up for my rights. My new beard – brown, flecked with red and gold – was staying put. Instead, I posed for a new passport photograph.

'How many days will you be in Czechoslovakia?' the consular official asked.

'Five,' I replied.

Inside the Tupolev, streamers of condensed air obfuscated the fuselage. I shivered, wrapped my overcoat around my shoulders, deepening the disguise. But that didn't fool passport control at Prague.

'This is not you,' the officer said. My accuser ran a finger over the plastic film that protected the photograph, as if to demonstrate how crude a forgery it was. He summoned his boss, who sported a natty mohair suit in place of regulation khaki. Both men stood in the cubicle comparing me with my photograph. They shook their heads. Had I undergone a metamorphosis during the flight to Kafka's city? I touched my face and the unfamiliar hair on my cheek made me start. At which the officer and his superior exchanged smiles. My passport was stamped.

Outside Airport Ruzyne I looked for a taxi. All I managed was a Skoda with a one-eyed driver.

'Hotel Ambassador,' I said.

'You are American?' the driver asked.

'Yes,' I said.

'You want to make money change?' he asked.

'No,' I said.

'Everyone makes money change,' he said.

'I don't need more currency,' I said.

'Here everyone needs more money,' he said. 'Since August all prices have risen one hundred per cent. How many crowns did you get to the dollar? Ten? I give you fifty.'

'No,' I said.

'Why not?' he asked. 'You change your dollars to crowns with me, then back again at the bank. You speculate, you make profit. Then you buy your wife a special present.'

'I am not married,' I said.

'I am not surprised,' he replied. Our conversation ended. Eventually our journey did too.

The woman at the hotel reception said: 'Please feel at home, Mr Smolinsky.' But Room 232 was un-American; there were brass pipes, an ancient telephone, and a single-channel radio that couldn't be unplugged (Miriam's ideas were not news in Czechoslovakia). But where was she?

Miriam didn't recognize me at once.

'It's the beard,' I said.

'Feldman sent you?' she asked.

I shrugged. 'You're still his wife,' I said. We were standing in the porch of the Staronova Synagogue. Miriam was a Jewish girl, it was Friday night, where else should I look?

'There's someone you'd better meet,' she said. His face – made distinctive by an eye-patch – was familiar. 'Tom Svoboda,' said Miriam, 'this is Joshua Smolinsky.'

We sat side by side before the *almemor*, above which hung the venerable banner of the Jewish community. Miriam joined the women at the back. Many seats remained empty, including the throne of the miracle-working Rabbi Low. My *siddur* was dedicated to the *shul* by Mimi Goldfarb of Nogales, Arizona. Tom seemed familiar with the Hebrew text. He prayed beautifully. The cantor, on the *almemor*, poured white wine into a silver goblet. His mellifluous voice filled the *shul*. The light, diffused by the dust of decaying paper, vibrated. The ancient synagogue tapered like the flame on a candle. Old men swaddled in *tallisim* rocked over their prayer books. 'Come, my friend, to greet the bride,' they sang, 'let us welcome the Sabbath day.' As the Hebrew words flew heavenwards the community's flag trembled, only to fall slack again when the song was ended. Miriam smiled at Tom.

After the service my Czech co-religionists mobbed me, anxious to tell their troubles to an American visitor.

'What has brought you to Prague?' they inquired.

'I came to meet an old friend,' I said. 'We no longer see much of one another. I live in Los Angeles, my friend in –'

But Miriam silenced my revelation with a kiss. '*Shabat shalom*,' she said.

'Why the secrecy?' I asked.

'I'll explain outside,' she replied; 'walls have ears.'

Before the congregants departed they shook Tom's hand.

'Why is Tom so popular?' I asked.

'His family were famous free-thinkers,' Miriam replied. 'But Tom has rediscovered his Jewish identity. Naturally that has made him something of a hero.'

He showed me his ring; a *mogen david* made out of tiny blue and white beads. His fingers also were stained blue. The beadle locked the door, and slouched off into the hostile night. We followed, Miriam hand-in-hand with Tom, in the direction of the Hotel Ambassador.

'You are a stranger, Joshua,' said Miriam. 'Prague seems beautiful, the Jews friendly. But it is a façade. The Jewish community is dying, and it is a metaphor for Prague. Stay around the synagogue long enough and each member will approach you with the news that the others are not to be trusted. Everyone's an informer. Not because they are loyal to the state – God forbid – but because they all want to be big-shots. If it got out that I was from Israel I'd have no peace. They'd all be trying to trick me into spreading Zionist propaganda, so as to have something meaty to report. That's how the government works. By bringing out the worst in people. These aren't Jews, they're kulaks.'

'Isn't that a bit harsh?' I said. 'What right have we to criticize?'

'Do not judge others, eh, Joshua?' said Miriam. 'I hope you'll be as reasonable tomorrow morning when I marry Tom.'

We dined in my hotel beneath an electric chandelier.

'Isn't bigamy a crime in Czechoslovakia?' I asked.

'Only if you're caught,' replied Miriam. 'Are you going to inform on us, Joshua?'

Tom solved my dilemma thus; he tapped his eye-patch. 'I see no husband,' he said.

Not far away, surrounded by waitresses in national costume, were the remains of Czechoslovakia. Banners were draped across the walls; they repeated, in many languages, the slogan of *Tourfilm '79*: 'Universal Peace and Understanding through Tourism.' The dining-room was chock-a-block with fraternal delegates from friendly countries. None more friendly than the Russians, of course. It was the Russians, resembling grotesque runners-up from Movie Mogul and Marilyn Monroe look-alike contests, who were chiefly responsible for the deteriorating condition of Czechoslovakia, formerly a giant liver paté in the shape of the Republic. Tom, however, ate nothing.

'Those Russian pigs have spoilt my appetite,' he said.

'Tom is a dissident,' whispered Miriam.

'I merely recognize that a radical change in the socio-political system is vital,' he said. 'At the same time I also know that it is completely out of the question.'

In the background, while a dance band played hit tunes of the 30s and 40s, Czechoslovakia finally disappeared.

Tom plucked a little tin from his pocket. It contained pink pills. 'Amphetamines,' he said.

'Tom takes them every Friday night,' explained Miriam, 'so he can work through the weekend without sleep.'

He popped a couple into his mouth, and a few more into a passing gravy-boat bound for the Russians. 'Soon they'll be higher than a sputnik,' he said.

When our roast duck arrived Tom tipped his portion into his napkin. 'I'll eat it later,' he said. He poured some vodka. 'I don't suppose I made a good impression the first time we met,' he said. 'Cab drivers are meant to be guides, not unofficial bankers. But for me to speak of the beauty of Prague would be a blasphemy. I no longer can see it. My eye-patch is a symbol. My eye is good. I wish to imitate our one-eyed national hero, Jan Zizka of Trocnov. Every twenty-crown note bears Zizka's portrait. I'll show you.'

He flattened a grubby bill on the table-cloth, revealing the hero's grim visage. 'Tell me,' he said, 'which eye is covered?'

'The right,' I replied.

'If you look in the back of Ctibor Rybar's *Guide to Prague* you'll also find a picture of Zizka,' said Tom. 'Only now the patch is over his left eye. What do you make of that?'

'Does it matter?' I said.

'Maybe Zizka was a bluffer like me,' he continued, 'who could never remember which eye was dud. Perhaps the printer was careless and reproduced Zizka back-to-front; such errors are not uncommon in Czechoslovakia. Or did our government order the change for political reasons? This is not far-fetched. Just last month the Kremlin discovered that two times two does not always make four. Naturally our government came to the same conclusion. Moreover they found a practical application for the new formula; our latest five-year plan must now be completed in four years. Two plus two equals five. The posters are all over Prague.'

'Is it safe to talk like this in public?' I asked.

Tom laughed.

'Nowhere's safer than here,' he said, nodding at the Russians. Whereupon the lights went out.

A false spring flourished. Bucolic images fluttered from projector to screen. *Tourfilm '79* began with the Czech entry. Steel workers were shown sweating over a furnace like demons in hell, then sent back-packing into the hills of Zdar. 'Motion recreation,' said the narrator, 'is their reward.'

'They think they can turn our countryside into a convalescent area,' hissed Tom, 'but they are fools!'

The camera overtook the hikers and swept down the hills of Zdar into the fertile valleys where peasants grew plums and apples. 'In the 1920s a group of artists left Prague to work amongst these communities,' said the voice-over. 'The spirit of the peasants gave new life to their paintings, and to Czech art, which was wallowing in self-conscious decadence. Foremost among them was Yehuda Svoboda, shown here in the traditional peasant costume he adopted.' An old photograph flickered into life.

'My uncle,' said Tom. 'How I worshipped him when I was a boy! What stories he used to tell! Oh, he loved "the spirit of the peasants". It had a name: slivovitz. The local whore fell in love with him. She was quite a celebrity; she had such a fund of foul language that professors and anthropologists would flock down just to hear her swear. She wore nothing but boots and a schoolboy's cap. My uncle painted her many times. He would pose her with a prop, say an umbrella, but exclude it from the picture. He said this was like most human activity, where the motive is also invisible.' A fanfare interrupted Tom.

'With renewed vigour we will achieve our goals!' cried the narrator. 'Two plus two equals five!'

'Fuck their slogans,' said Tom. 'We'll free two times two! Let two times two equal a bunch of bananas. Victory to the irrational! We call the children of our leaders "Banana Kids". Because only the elite eat bananas in Czechoslovakia. I want a banana!'

Tom jumped up. And we all departed to the sound of wind breaking from bloated bellies, as Czech cooking took its revenge upon the Russian constitution.

Beneath the moonlight pornography thrived. Beside the Vlatava, four mallards were raping a duck. She had been flattened into the mud, as if awaiting the butcher's knife. One after another the drakes rode her back, while the others stabbed at her neck. Her body shuddered, torn between pleasure and pain. Her arteries throbbed, at bursting point. She shrieked.

'Motion recreation,' I said.

'Rape!' cried Miriam.

'Shoo,' I said. To no avail.

'Tom,' yelled Miriam, 'do something!'

Better acquainted with the psychology of the locals he emptied his pockets in search of his uneaten dinner. He tore off several lumps of meat and threw them in the mêlée. The effect was immediate. Female flesh was abandoned in favour of the cooked variety. Gobbling, squabbling, the mallards cleaned up. They pecked at our shoes, quacking for more.

'Cannibals,' said Miriam.

'No,' said Tom, 'just good Czech ducks.'

Tom lived in a large block opposite the Staronova Synagogue. It was dated 1911 and decorated in the style of that period: golden profiles impressed upon glossy green tiles. The figures were of sleek men and sporting girls characterized by boxing gloves and tennis racquets. One face alone did not fit. A hook-nosed caricature. For those unfamiliar with skull-caps and earlocks, a money bag, a pile of ducats and a *mogen david* had been added. I was startled by the impression that the Jew had turned to face me, but it was only a man – equally Jewish – looking down from a window above.

'Don't stare,' advised Miriam. 'The authorities are very clever. They know visiting Jews will be outraged by that anti-semitic insult. So they have installed a spy in the building. He photographs everyone who stops to look at it.'

'But the man at the window was a Jew,' I said.

'Don't let that fool you,' replied Miriam.

Tom unlocked the door of his apartment with a silver key that hung from a leather thong around his neck. His room resembled a bazaar. He had boxes overflowing with jeans, tee-shirts, eye-patches, beads and rings; shelves filled with banned books and magazines. In the centre stood a hand printing press, surrounded by bottles of ink in shades of blue. Hanging from strings that looped from wall to wall were scores of 20-crown notes.

'Oh, my God!' I exclaimed. 'You're a forger!'

'No,' explained Miriam, 'Tom's an artist.'

'The printing press belonged to my uncle,' he said, 'and I think he'd approve of its new function. In Czechoslovakia crime has become an art form, because real art is illegal. I am a criminal – it is true – but an artist also. Tomorrow, after the wedding, I will give you a demonstration. We will have a small happening. You will come?'

'Please,' added Miriam.

I softened, but did not melt. 'Shouldn't dissent be non-profit-making?' I inquired.

'The money I earn on the black market saves me from being a slave of the system,' said Tom. 'I fell in love with Miriam when I heard her play Dvořák's violin concerto in the House of Artists. I didn't block my ears because Dvořák exchanged a pittance in Prague for a fortune in America.'

Miriam picked up the fiddle that had won Tom's heart and began to play. Instead of the melancholy cadences of the mercenary composer I heard the disciplined cacophony of a revolutionary. Composition was the talent the printing press financed.

'All my compositions are based upon the dodecaphonic serial technique developed by Schönberg,' Tom said. 'Variety is obtained by repeating the series either in retrograde or inversion or even retrograde inversion, giving me twenty-four, thirty-six or forty-eight variables.'

Such explanations did not impress Tom's neighbour, who cut short the recital by thumping on the wall.

'That's our spy,' said Tom. 'He knows my work is banned.'

Forgive me, Feldman. But what could I do? Have them arrested? We were in the waiting-room of the Old Town Hall. The ornate woodwork buzzed with the sound of a distant organ. A panel opened and a woman aglitter with black diamanté appeared.

'You have an English translation of the wedding ceremony?' she asked.

Miriam showed her papers, each with its official stamp of approval, including the document that proved she was single.

'How did you do it?' I asked.

'Bribery,' she replied. 'I can tell you exactly what each seal cost. The cheapest was a bag of coffee, the most expensive took 200 dollars.' As we entered the wedding chamber the organ began to play the Israeli national anthem.

'They could hardly object to Smetana's *Vltava*,' said Miriam.

The Deputy Mayor for Marriages picked up a large leather folder and pronounced the vows. When he had finished Miriam said, 'Yes.'

They posed for photographs beneath the astrological clock. A small crowd had gathered around Tom's cab, with its tell-tale white ribbons, among whom were some whose occupation was obvious. Nevertheless, Tom had his happening. He threw handfuls of home-made 20-crown bills at the sky. They swirled upwards like giant pieces of confetti, while Miriam performed Stravinsky's *The Devil's Dance*. There was a commotion as masses flocked from the four corners of the square like pigeons scenting food. The music progressed faster and faster through its dizzying harmonies, until the people were possessed by its rhythms and began leaping into the air after the drifting notes. High above our heads the horologe chimed noon, as the skeleton pulled the bell-rope in his niche. This activated the apostles who appeared in the upper windows of the clock; it also prompted the secret policemen who began to move towards us.

'Time we vanished,' said Tom.

We resurfaced near Holesov, not far from the Polish border. On the outskirts a blond officer in a blue uniform stood beside the road, a pair of binoculars in his hand. As we approached he lifted them to his eyes and examined us like a voyeur who had no need for secrecy.

'If anyone asks,' said Tom over his shoulder, 'you're a couple of American tourists.'

We checked into the Hotel Savoy; a single room for Tom, and a double for me and Miriam.

'What a way to spend your honeymoon,' I said.

Next morning the manager handed Tom a message. 'We must remain here a few days,' he announced.

On the third day the manager returned my passport. 'I am sorry,' he said, 'but you cannot stay another night.' My visa had expired early It was the consular official's revenge.

'There is a simple solution,' remarked Tom.

'You have made many problems for me,' said the manager, pocketing my 50-dollar bill. Holesov had only one place nobody paid a bribe to get into.

Washing was drying on the gates of the old Jewish cemetery; beyond was evidence of the Nazis' dirty linen. If it wasn't for a plaque commemorating the extinct Jewish community an ignorant stranger might have concluded that the Jews had discovered the secret of eternal life, for no new tombstone had been put up in forty years. A man was tending a fertile little garden.

'You wish to know about the Yiddish people?' he asked. 'I am not

Yiddish, but I knew them. I was their *shabbos goy*. They were kind to me, but they drove their rabbis away. One was sacked for being too strict over matters of ritual slaughter, another left because he believed that he could do his job better than his congregation, and a third resigned after a dispute about priestly blessings. They were still quarrelling when the Germans arrived.'

He led us through tall grass, disturbing the crickets, past the victims of a milder epidemic – a pogrom – back in time to the seventeenth-century tomb of Rabbi Shabatai Cohen. The inscription, of course, was in Hebrew.

'What does it say?' asked our guide. 'There is no one left in Holesov who can read it.'

I coughed, Miriam blushed, Tom walked away. The phoney! His Hebrew was no better than mine. He settled beneath a plum tree, where he attached himself to a couple who had wandered through the open gate.

'This one was a farmer who gave us milk,' continued our guide, introducing us to the tombstones. 'That one's daughter was secretary to Jan Masaryk, this one was our doctor, that one our dentist.'

Suddenly Miriam sprinted towards Tom, as money changed hands. 'Liar! Defiler!' she screamed.

'Excuse me,' I said to our perplexed guide.

Under the plum tree Miriam and Tom were having their first row.

'Joshua,' yelled Miriam, 'I've married a man who sells forged concentration-camp stamps in Jewish graveyards!'

'What harm have I done?' said Tom.

'None, none,' shouted Miriam. 'We'll go to Auschwitz next. You can hawk soap there!'

'My wife, the actress,' said Tom. He opened his wallet to reveal some more examples of the offending article. They illustrated delightful rural scenes, with leafy trees and rivers meandering down from rounded hills. Below was the single word: 'Theresienstadt'.

'You should enter them in *Tourfilm '79*,' I said.

Tom laughed. He reached up into the heavy branches that drooped over his head and picked some of the dusty purple fruit. 'Have one,' he said.

'No, thanks,' I replied.

'Too squeamish, eh?' said Tom. He squeezed the plums between his fingers until the skin cracked and the stone was exposed. Then he sucked in the flesh. His lips became sticky with juice.

'You're disgusting,' said Miriam.

That night four strangers showed up at the Hotel Savoy asking for Tom. They looked like smugglers, but he introduced them as Polish dissidents. We went upstairs into the double room.

'Have you heard the latest?' asked one of the Poles. 'Brezhnev visits a pig-farm in Poland. The journalists crowd around him taking photographs. Next day the pictures are in all the papers. The captions say: "Yesterday Mr Brezhnev was photographed with Polish pigs. Mr Brezhnev is the one on the left."'

The dissidents roared with laughter. They opened bottles marked 'Czysta Wodka Wyborowa' and passed them around. One bottle, however, had no label. Its contents tasted medicinal rather than alcoholic.

'What's this?' I asked.

'Brezhnev's piss,' said someone.

Is this why we waited four days in Holesov, for a good laugh at the Kremlin's expense? Miriam, though drunk, was still angry with Tom. When he asked her to play the violin for his friends she refused.

'Miriam,' he said, 'they have come all the way from Cracow to hear my latest composition.' She shook her head. Without warning Tom slapped her round the face. 'Play, you bitch,' he said.

'You don't have to,' I said.

'It's all right, Joshua,' she said. 'I'll play.'

Perhaps Tom's friends were genuine for they seemed to find something to appreciate in the dreadful music. Anyway, they scribbled in notepads from beginning to end. And when Miriam finished they applauded. One even kissed her hand.

'I am tired,' she said. 'I'll rest for a while in the other room.'

I accompanied her. We sat on the bed. I put my arm around her shoulder.

'Disillusioned?' I said.

She nodded, and began to sob. 'What am I going to do, Joshua?' she asked.

However, I was anxious to answer a different question: what was so important about Tom's music? 'Miriam, what if those Poles haven't come to listen to the music as music,' I said, 'but as something else?'

'What else can music be?' she said.

'A message,' I replied. 'Tom uses notes in a fixed series. Suppose he gave each note an alphabetical value, wouldn't it be possible to transmit a message?'

'I guess so,' said Miriam.

Twenty minutes later we had the first sentence: 'The medicine has been ordered and is on its way.'

I was trapped in a lunatic plot, but the country outside was no more sane. In cracking Tom's code I had been dropped unprepared into his world; the doors of perception were open and I was dazzled by the light. Something was happening, that was for sure. I looked at Miriam, beside me on the bed, and saw only satellites of colour. Nothing was still, including my senses. Miriam began to hum. The tune concealed a message. It said, 'Kiss me.'

I must have been mad, making it with the bigamous wife of my old friend on her second honeymoon. But I unbuttoned her whilst she unzipped me. Like mindless marionettes we performed for the secret police, four or five of them. It was not the doors of perception that had been broken down, but the door of my room; I was not blinded by revelation, but by the flashlights of the cops. They seemed very upset. So did Miriam.

'*Nemluvim cesky!*' she screamed. '*Americky konzulat!*' However, it was not difficult to decipher the meaning in our visitors' presence – 'You are under arrest.' In my illogical state I thought it was because I had just fucked Miriam.

The room was small. I needed neither passport nor visa to enter it. My identity was not in doubt, only my continuing existence outside the room. Who will send a Joshua Smolinsky to look for me? The room contained two chairs and one desk. I was in the chair on the wrong side of the desk. My interrogator, opposite, looked like Otto Preminger's wicked brother.

'Mr Svoboda has confessed to everything,' he said.

'Then why do you need to question me?' I replied.

'For your own good,' he said. 'The courts are easier on those who confess.'

I kept it to myself, but I was not sure why Tom had been arrested. Were his sins political or criminal? My interrogator, however, was a mind-reader.

'Your friend is a forger and a drug smuggler,' he said. 'In fact you sampled one of his products this evening. I have been told that you found it quite potent. What you drank was a condensed concoction of poppy juice. The kids call it *soup*. You see, Mr Smolinsky, nature has played a dirty trick on Poland. She has blessed its fields with the opium poppy. Of course it is impossible for the authorities to prevent peasants and students from collecting the unripe heads. These are your precious dissidents. They pretend to be composers, poets, idealists; but in reality they are nothing but drug dealers who corrupt our youth. Nevertheless, I have no doubt that Tom Svoboda will be turned into a hero by your Western press.'

'You have only yourselves to blame for that,' I said.

'Mrs Feldman thought Svoboda was a dissident, she admired him, but you thought he was a crook?' he said.

'Correct,' I said.

'So why didn't you report him?' he asked.

'Because he was a friend of a friend,' I replied.

'Rubbish!' he said. 'What do you know of loyalty? Perhaps now and again, through circumstances beyond our control, we have betrayed the revolution – but you! Why, less than three hours ago you were making a fool of the man you call your friend, and a mockery of the contract between you. No doubt you consider yourself my moral superior. What could be lower in the eyes of an American than a Czechoslovakian secret policeman? But I spit on your morality, you self-righteous hypocrite! Tell me the truth! Why were you travelling with Tom Svoboda? What is the connection between the CIA and the opium trade?'

I repeated my story. He was not impressed.

'Confess,' says the rabbi. 'Being stiff-necked will do our people no good.'

'Rabbi,' I say, 'does two times two always equal four?'

The rabbi, evidently a scholar of the cabbala, thinks for a minute. 'Not always,' he responds, 'for example, two eggs plus two tomatoes make a Spanish omelette.'

My drugged senses rebel. The naked light bulb explodes, scattering shards of light. A rustling sound comes from the jagged hole as streams of angels and gargoyles pour forth, filling the room with the scent of cinnamon and dung. The gargoyles attach themselves to my beard and hair.

'See,' says the rabbi, 'this is what happens to those who do not repent.'

I crack. But before I can speak my guardian angel lands upon my shoulder and folds a wing over my mouth. 'I've got someone I want you to meet,' he says.

A black-haired man steps forward and walks towards me across the splinters of light.

'Joshua Smolinsky,' says my guardian angel, 'this is Miklós Radnóti. Miklós was a poet. The Nazis killed him. He was a hero, not a counterfeit like Tom. When his body was exhumed after the war a notebook was found in his coat pocket. It contained his last poems. Listen to "Letter to my wife".'

Miklós Radnóti reads:

> 'I once believed in miracles – now though
> I forget their dates . . . Above me bombers go . . .
> I was just admiring your eyes' blue in the sky,
> But clouds came and a plane up there flew by
> With bombs longing to fall. A prisoner,
> I live despite them. All I have hopes for
> I've thought out, yet I'll find my way to you.
> For I have walked the soul's full length for you –
> And the roads of all these lands; through scarlet ash
> I'll charm my way if need be, through the crash
> Of worlds on fire – and yet I shall get back.
> If need be, I'll be tough as a tree's bark;
> And the calm that hardened men have, who each hour
> Know danger, stress – a calm worth guns and power –
> Soothes me and, like a cool wave of the sea,
> Sobering, "two-times-two" breaks over me.'

'I'm going to give you some advice,' says my guardian angel. 'I admit that I'm a flop when it comes to making up plots – if my original script hadn't been so lousy it wouldn't have been burnt and Feldman wouldn't have a cinder in his eye and you wouldn't be in this mess now – but I do know right from wrong. When all else fails, judge a man by his heroes. Tom may be worthless, but he's still better than his rulers. After all, *svoboda* means freedom.'

'Well?' says my interrogator.

The wing lifts from my mouth. I repeat the last lines of 'Letter to my Wife'. There is applause. It comes from the interface of my cheek and the interrogator's hand. He hits me once, twice, three times . . . until I lose count and consciousness.

I wake up in a cell. It is dark, I am cold. I do not wash, I eat only potatoes. A bucket in a corner fills with my urine and shit. But I do not confess. After a number of days they let me out. I am being deported, that is all I am told. Miriam is also at the airport.

'Thank God!' she cries.

'Same flight?' I ask.

Miriam nods. 'I've decided to give Feldman one more chance,' she says. 'Your face . . .'

'It's my beard,' I say. 'I felt so dirty when they released me that I shaved it off.'

Our flight to the States is called. The man at the desk looks at my passport photograph and looks at me. 'This is not you,' he says. 'Until you grow a beard you cannot leave the country.'

'Poor Joshua,' says Miriam. 'I'll give your regards to Feldman.'

She disappears among the crowd in the departure lounge. I take a taxi back to Prague. My driver wears an eye patch. 'You want to make money change?' he asks.

'Why are you free?' I ask.

'They decided I was harmless, no threat to the state,' says Tom, 'indeed, a valuable source of hard currency.'

We stop in a shadowy alley around the corner from the Hotel Ambassador. I hand over 100 dollars. He counts out 5,000 crowns; eight 500-crown bills, each bearing two Second World War soldiers, and fifty 20-crown notes.

'Don't worry,' he says, 'they're genuine.'

In my room I check the money. It doesn't add up. There are no soldiers, only Zizka glaring at me out of his one good eye.

Tsatske

Ask Adam about women! Or better yet, let me tell you about my wife.

We were both illegal immigrants. I was smuggled in by the Professor, my wife by the Professor's father-in-law. The Professor found me in the Gesia cemetery. Warsaw, Poland. Limbless, fleshless, I used my head — what else has a Jew got? — to burrow to the surface. And there I remained until a summer shower left my cranium as shiny as a silk *yarmulkah*. Thank God, I caught the Professor's eye, in which a tear formed. Moved beyond words, he snatched my skull from the reluctant earth.

Then followed the posthumous realization of my life-long dream: the escape to America — although I nearly gave the game away at the airport when I intoned the prayer for starting a journey from the depths of the Professor's satchel. Fortunately no one heard me; except, perhaps, the Almighty.

My new life was luxurious, but I was lonely, I desired to be uxorious. I dwelt upon a filing-cabinet in the Professor's study, so that I could see over his shoulder as he typed his lectures and his letters. His wife bathed me regularly in milk. Thus I derived intellectual sustenance, plus not a little nourishment. But I longed for a companion in a similar predicament, someone with whom I could share intimate secrets. Sex was out of the question, of course, but I would not refuse a kiss. I dreamed of lips, female lips. 'Send me someone to love,' I prayed. And God listened.

Now the Professor's father-in-law was an oil-man, and he made many journeys to South America. Returning from one such expedition up the Pastaza river in darkest Ecuador, he crept into the Professor's study like an anarchist. You would have thought his briefcase contained a bomb. Instead he pulled out a woman's head no bigger than a monkey's. The Professor's father-in-law recounted how he had encountered the fierce Jivaros, who turned out to be friendly after all. So much so that they gave each member of the party a shrunken head as a keepsake. 'The Indians called them *tsantsas*,' he explained. He knew that it was forbidden to export such cultural artefacts, and used that as an excuse to leave the unwelcome present with his hosts in

Quito. But when he was passing through Customs he put his hand in his jacket pocket and felt the shrunken features of my intended.

We were ideally matched: I was a skull with no face, she was a face with no skull. That's how the Jivaros do it; out comes the skull, in goes hot sand. The Professor and his father-in-law examined my future wife beneath the reading lamp. Her black hair had lost none of its natural sheen, nor her full lips any of their sensuousness. Unmistakably the lips of my dream, even though they were sewn together with catgut.

'She should be in a museum,' said the Professor.

'What provenance do I give?' replied his father-in-law.

Since when did Providence require provenance? So they left her beside me upon the filing-cabinet. A curiosity to them, a Godsend to me. A *tsantsas* to the Indians, a *tsatske* to me. My brainless cutie.

So what if she was a *shiksa*? It was too late for me to worry about such niceties. At first our conversation was somewhat limited. I asked questions in Yiddish, she replied in Jivaran. But like the greenhorns of old, she soon picked up a smattering of English. We conducted our courtship in secret. Who knew if our fragile relationship could withstand the publicity our oracular abilities would inevitably occasion? Eventually I proposed, and she accepted.

'Will you have me?' I asked.

'I will,' she replied.

That was enough, we were married.

By chance our wedding-night was enlivened by a jazz-band ball. The Professor and his wife had a visitor, a colleague of the Professor's. The two men retired to the study, lately our boudoir, to discuss university business. Meanwhile the Professor's wife washed up the dinner plates in the kitchen. It so happened their apartment was designed by an architect who equated privacy with repression, as a consequence of which all groans, squeaks, giggles, whispers, tinkles and plops carried to every corner. The two men were deep in earnest conversation when my saviour's wife looked in to say goodnight.

'I've a migraine,' she said. 'I'm going to bed.'

Shortly afterwards, the Professor learned that he and his colleague shared a passion: jazz. As if by magic, records appeared; louder and louder soared the cornet and the clarinet.

'The bastard,' whispered my partner; 'is he trying to drive his wife crazy?'

I squirmed. Even the Professor's colleague seemed uncomfortable.

Only the Professor was surprised when the festivities were terminated by a dreadful scream. And we were left alone while tempers flared elsewhere.

'We'll never get like that,' said my wife. She rubbed her hair against my sunken cheek.

Who said mixed marriages don't work?

To increase my stone-age spouse's understanding of the modern world I started to read the Professor's lectures to her as he was typing them. And that's when our troubles began.

'My name is not Rothschild,' he wrote, 'but I am a banker. President of the Jewish Moral Bank. Our assets include six million dead since 1939, not to mention countless millions in earlier crusades, inquisitions and pogroms. All a customer has to do is prove his Jewish identity and the benefits of our group membership will be his immediately: *carte blanche* to sit in judgement on any subject that takes his fancy. And don't worry if you're not Jewish; women, pygmies, blacks need not feel excluded. Provided your ancestors have suffered sufficiently you can behave as badly as you like and still claim moral superiority.'

He paused. His mind was elsewhere. Suddenly he abandoned his lecture, placed a clean piece of paper in his typewriter and composed a passionate letter to the wife of his colleague.

'The hypocrite,' hissed my wife through her stitched lips.

'You don't know the facts,' I said, 'how can you pass judgement?'

'Because I am a woman,' she replied.

Did I mention that before the Nazis shot me for stealing a loaf of bread I was a wealthy man?

My *tsatske* never forgave me for that. 'You suffered for a year or two,' she said, 'but I was a slave all my life.'

The Jivaros were generally chivalrous when it came to shrinking heads, my wife being a rare exception. Her crime? She complained too much. Hence the catgut, *pour encourager les autres*. Pity she didn't learn from her mistake. She screamed for the Professor's wife, alternating the word 'adultery'.

There are times when secrecy is more important than discovery, as the Professor well knew. Ignoring our miraculous qualities, he dumped us both on the compost heap at the bottom of the garden. Here we blame one another for our fall. Jays nest in my head. Eggs hatch, birds fly, but our argument is eternal.

Kayn Aynhoreh

I have never been on particularly good terms with my organs. What a querulous bunch they are; my kidneys remind me of those scruffy malcontents you see outside urinals selling socialist newspapers, while my liver is even more bolshevik, dedicated to overthrowing the system altogether. I wasn't more than three or four when they began to rebel, ordering bladder and bowel to bully my sphincters. My spirit was strong, but my sphincters were weak. They defected and I defecated. To deprive the offending organs of sustenance I stopped eating. Food was masticated until my cheeks were full, whereupon I deposited the soggy balls in a handkerchief. Sick of soiled underwear my mother took me to a famous paediatrician. Before she could open her mouth he spoke:

'Please, Mrs Silkstone, no symptoms! Allow me to divine why you're here. Information is an insult to my profession.'

'Jonah doesn't . . .' began my mother.

'We don't need a witchdoctor to know that your son doesn't eat,' continued the paediatrician. 'He looks like he spent his summer holidays at Belsen.'

In fact we went to Bournemouth, where my parents had to endure the disapproving stares of the other holiday-makers as I tottered around like a new-born giraffe. One old *bubbe* actually approached my mother and whispered in her ear:

'To me it looks like your boy's got atavism. Just like my poor sister Feigele, God rest her soul. One night our great-grandmother came in a dream to her. "Feigele," she said, "would it kill you just once to visit my grave?" But Feigele was too full of life. She forgot about the cemetery. So she was punished. She got a blockage, and starved to death. That's what the doctors call atavism.'

But the paediatrician could find nothing wrong with me. 'An obstinate bugger,' he observed. 'Forget *cogito ergo sum*, my son, or you'll end up on an intravenous drip.'

'God forbid!' shrieked my mother.

'Don't worry, Mrs Silkstone,' added the paediatrician, 'he's a healthy lad.' Unversed in Latin, my mother made the appropriate Yiddish response.

It is common among my tribe to supplement any compliment with the phrase '*kayn aynhoreh*', especially when the recipient of praise is a child. Thus when the midwife held me by my feet and said, 'It's a bonny boy,' my mother quickly added:

'*Kayn aynhoreh.*'

'A strange name,' muttered the midwife.

'I'm not naming him,' replied my mother, 'I'm warding off the evil eye.' Deflected, it struck elsewhere. Wriggling like Houdini trapped inside a body several sizes too small I made the midwife drop her thermometer. It smashed on contact with the ground, releasing a swarm of invisible insects with milky eyes. A delivery from Mercury, messenger of the gods, but what was the message?

As if I knew. I am innocent! Fat difference that made. Look what happened when my mother left me supine in my perambulator, absorbing vitamins from the sunshine. Every so often a neighbour's face would rise like a premature moon and utter these words: 'Don't look so worried, it may never happen.' Can a baby be held responsible for its expression?

Even worse was the attitude of my creative director. One fine morning his bovine secretary summoned me to the chief's office. This was not unexpected. I had been producing good advertisements without much thanks. Restitution was about to be made.

'Jonah,' said the creative director, 'there is no easy way to tell you this.' Not the traditional method of announcing a promotion. On the contrary, I was being sacked.

'It's not your work,' he said. 'It's your manner. Where's your enthusiasm? To tell you the truth, no one wants to be your copywriter. And I don't blame them. Whenever I see your gloomy face I go into an immediate depression. Do you know something I don't? Can't you ever smile?'

He went so far as to accuse me of bringing bad luck upon the agency. Me – the evil eye! When my whole life had been a struggle against it. The evil eye can attack your organs or your luck. If it attacks your organs it is called a virus. Viruses are one of the risks of social intercourse. Colds, cancers, venereal diseases – all are souvenirs of a stranger's room or another's pants. Always say '*kayn aynhoreh*' before you leave and wash when you return. Needless to report, sex is one of the evil eye's greatest allies. Who can predict the consequences of an involvement with that siren? For example, my puberty nearly killed my parents.

Without warning one bath-night, sticky dew appeared where only pee had previously passed. Henceforth baths were taken in Y-fronts, within which my penis lurked like a pebble in a catapult. If only I had worn them in bed. Instead I kissed my *mezuzah*. Some prophylactic! I borrowed this ritual from my father who invariably kissed his fingers and touched the *mezuzah* on his door-jamb before retiring. If it worked for him why didn't it do the trick for me? I never saw my father hide his pyjama trousers at the bottom of the laundry basket. What was the secret? To find the answer I removed my father's *mezuzah* from its bracket and prised open the back with a fingernail to reveal a tiny roll of parchment no bigger than a cigarette. Replacing the empty *mezuzah*, I returned to bed with the scroll. Hebrew characters were inscribed therein, which I recognized but did not understand, although I knew them to be potent medicine – so potent that without their protection my mother and father fell victim to influenza simultaneously. Shame-faced I let the doctor in on the secret of its cause.

'Foolish boy,' he guffawed. 'Years ago everyone was as silly as you. They blamed influenza upon the malign influence of the stars. Hence its name. Nowadays we know influenza is a virus. A virus is a poison that tells fibs to your cells – that's what bodies are made of. So the cells misbehave and you get ill.' Like everyone else the doctor mistook my expression. 'Don't worry,' he said, 'your parents will soon be on their feet again, *kayn aynhoreh*.'

But not before they almost died, as I said. However, I was not anticipating that delirium; I was evaluating my new knowledge. Lulled by the robustness of adolescence I had let my organs develop unchecked for far too long, allowed the evil eye to take advantage of the structure of protoplasm and set up a network of terrorist cells dedicated to toppling the status quo and giving my body a mind of its own. Thereafter, whenever I strolled through a fairground and saw the children swirling down a helter-skelter I could only think of how one virus or another was doing exactly the same with my deoxyribonucleic acid!

I want you to know that I am as familiar with psychoanalytic dicta as I am with new developments in microbiology. Orthodox Freudians explain psychosomatic illnesses as a defence mechanism against the secret desire to transgress taboos such as incest. I should be so lucky! My body is part of a conspiracy to stop me growing up. I struggle to become independent, it craves dependency. I have already referred to my dismissal from the advertising agency where I was an art director. That was merely the latest in a long line of artistic triumphs.

Thus far my achievements are these: I have more ears than Van Gogh and I am taller than Toulouse-Lautrec. Ever since I can remember I wanted to be an artist. A few weeks after my *bar mitzvah* I set my bedroom curtains alight. I had been throwing fireworks through an open window into the darkness, hypnotized by the golden arcs they described, when a spark touched the chaste veil the middle class likes to have between itself and the outside world. Just one spark was all it took to send the tulle equivalent of *kayn aynhoreh* up in flames. Frantically my parents went to work with wet towels, while I felt as light-headed as Prometheus unbound. Here was prophecy! Not only would I destroy the middle-class values that were smothering artistic expression, but I would also liberate the living spirits that were trapped within even tulle. Unfortunately, the house was saved. Nevertheless, I recorded the incident with my coloured pencils. I was merely testing my brightest orange by pressing its point against my fingertip when our au-pair, who was fumigating my bedroom with Air-wick to remove the last vestiges of smoke, cried out: 'Jonah, be careful!'

'Of what?' I asked.

So she told me about lead poisoning. How an insignificant scratch from a pencil could prove fatal.

'A red line moves from wound to heart,' she explained, 'causing death upon arrival.' She was the daughter of a doctor. Swiss, no less. Why should I doubt her? Subsequent drawings were all done with biro, ruining the spontaneity of my line for ever. But worse was to follow.

At the time I was still attending a private school in one of London's more genteel suburbs. It was perhaps the safest place in the world. The only evidence of change was provided by the cherry trees which dotted the pavement with blossom in the spring and with leaves in the autumn. This convinced the locals that time was circular, not linear, as a consequence of which they voted for the same Conservative Member of Parliament each general election. On the day of which I am speaking the cherry trees were bare. It was my last Christmas at St Martin's. Next term I would be making a late appearance at the local grammar school. But now my exams were all behind me, I could relax. I remember we were making paper-chains with which to festoon the ceiling. Each of us was given our own section which we would join with our neighbour's when both were completed. But I was a romantic, I wanted to link mine with Sarah Langer's, who was being sent to a girls' boarding school on the other side of England. So I walked across the classroom towards her, my arms filled with a chain as substantial as a rainbow. At the same time a small boy who had been sharpening a pencil carelessly raised his arm, and immediate pain replaced imagined pleasure. My ear! Stabbed with the poisonous tip. Sarah screamed as blood dripped from my lobe, an earring with ambitions to be a necklace. I was rushed to the nurse, who dabbed the wound with stinging disinfectant and assured me that the bleeding would soon cease. But that ruddy overflow was the last thing on my mind. I was thinking of that other red line racing for my heart. According to my religion, a *bar mitzvah* marks the attainment of majority. Here was I, not two months a man, already waiting for death!

Of course I didn't die. But I wasn't cured of my phobia either Maybe I wouldn't be so fortunate a second time. I had become a hypochondriac. The only disease I did not fear was breast cancer. So imagine my horror when I discovered lumps around my groin. Luckily I had recently been permitted to explore my girlfriend's genitalia with my fingers. As soon as was possible I took the opportunity, under the guise of passionate caresses, of checking her groin for similar nodules. Thank God she had them too. I was a student by then. And, tetanus notwithstanding, I played football for the university. Even so, I did not sever all my links with the suburb of my parents. I also kept goal for Wingate Football Club, when I had the time. If ever you drive north on the new motorway you'll pass over the remains of their ground. Where long-distance lorries now spray cars with mud I was once a hero, famous for my spectacular saves. It was as though my mind had some intuitive knowledge of which way the opposing forward was going to kick the ball. And in the glorious moment of connection I found an ideal image for my relationship with the world: a spinning globe captured with perfect grace. My stinging palms prophesied a brave future. How could it be otherwise when actuality so much resembled anticipation? I'll tell you.

I was high. I had just saved a penalty. Cheers still resounded in my ears. My fingers tingled as if eager to be at the paints again. After the match I doodled in the programme. Before long I had turned the team into an inverted pyramid with myself at the base. Then I became a circus acrobat supporting upon my shoulders two full-backs, three half-backs and five forwards. Next game I was tormented by the burden, and started to stagger under the weight of the responsibility. I lost confidence in my sense of balance. When I collected the ball from the back of the net for the sixth time, the spectators yelled that I was *shikker* – Wingate being the only Jewish team in the league. If only it were that simple. Who would believe that I had acrophobia at sea level? That afternoon my father walked home alone, as covered in shame as I was in mud. Returning to university I sought solace with my *shiksa*. I unbuttoned her blouse and began to fondle her breasts. The lump I discovered wasn't very big, but it was big enough. It just wasn't my day.

All things considered, my initial success in the world of advertising was something of a miracle. Yet I started off like a house on fire. I had long since learned that pencils were made of graphite, not lead, but it didn't matter either way, since art directors don't actually have to be able to draw. As you probably know, art directors and copywriters work as a team. I'll call my partner Iggy. Our first campaign was on behalf of a rather dull brand of whisky. We soon changed that image. It became 'The Whisky that Breaks all the Rules'. We went from success to success. Eventually the endless praise gripped my skull like a halo several sizes too small. I began to complain of headaches, which Iggy diagnosed as hangovers.

'Too much whisky,' he said. 'It's very unprofessional to believe your own advertisements, you know.'

Then, realizing at last the depth of my distress, Iggy began to play upon my fears. Not that it needed much persuasion to convince me of the infidelity of my organs. Who would they fall for? Syphilis, the demon lover? Polio, the hunchbacked smotherer? Diphtheria, the throat-slashing terrorist? Cancer, the vampire? Even worse than these were the diseases with unknown characters, invisible assassins who struck for no reason, whose only symptom was death. Medicine can offer no protection against the unannounced murderer. The only defence we have is *kayn aynhoreh*. I said it so many times that Iggy renamed me Ken. But it worked, until the agency entrusted us with their largest account.

The client wanted his whole range exposed. So we took the company name and transformed each letter into one of its products. The visuals would be animated, the commentary would begin: 'Every letter tells a story.' For example, 'O' was the door of a spin-dryer. As the whole machine was gradually revealed a woman's voice could be heard: 'Dear

Hotpoint, When Mrs Stegosaurus told me about her new spin-dryer I didn't believe her. Now I do, thanks to you.' Most commercials work on the principle of conversion by proxy, ours was no exception. All we lacked was a handsome presenter the buyers could trust, as our creative director pointed out.

'Where's the human touch?' he cried. 'Housewives like soft soap. We need men, not machines.'

Despite these objections, the campaign was presented to the client. I lacked the energy to make the introduction. Instead the task fell to an account executive, who lost his job as a result.

'Is this what you had in mind?' he inquired.

'Don't ask me!' stormed the client. 'I'm paying you to tell me!'

The following day the creative director put his hand on my shoulder. 'Bad news,' he said, 'I'm afraid we've lost it.' I tried to look glum, but so perverse was my face that it registered a smile. 'You mustn't blame yourself,' said the creative director.

I didn't, but Iggy did. Behind my back. It was he who complained of my lack of enthusiasm, it was he who asked to work with another art director. He saved his skin, but not mine. Three years later I was fired.

'Good luck, Ken,' said Iggy as I walked out of his life.

In the meantime I had entered that of Rosie Silverman. After our marriage we discovered that the only thing we had in common was a love of chocolate. But we didn't know that when we were courting. During those heady weeks we spent hours in bed not making love. At first I tried to disguise my impotence with whimsical tales which I spun out like Scheherazade, but there were limits even to Rosie's patience.

'What's the matter?' she asked. 'Don't you like me?'

I liked her, but the message wasn't reaching my loins, somewhere en route my libido was being sabotaged. We were both naked. It was Rosie's birthday and the remains of our feast were scattered around the room: pheasant bones, oyster shells, peach stones and a crystal bowl which still contained traces of a chocolate mousse.

'Eat me,' she said.

I was shocked; Rosie did not look the kind of woman who would make such a request. You must understand that although I was not a greenhorn, as you will recall, my experience was somewhat limited. She tasted like one of those sherbet dips I used to suck as a kid, but without the fizz. Afterwards she yawned and stretched her limbs like a satisfied

107

animal. As for my tongue, I wondered if it would ever fit back into my mouth.

'Now it's your turn,' said Rosie. Quick as a flash she spooned the chocolate mousse over my private parts. 'Right, Mr Silkstone,' she said, 'you're about to receive your just desserts.'

She buried her face in the mousse, and refused to take no for an answer. To my astonishment I heard myself groaning. Then I don't know what I did. Finally, with exquisite precision, I spat the burden of self into her mouth.

'There,' said Rosie, 'you're normal after all.'

Overwhelmed with gratitude I proposed. If sexual intercourse were only an adequate replacement for conversation we might have been happy.

Expelled from the agency, I was condemned to a life of solitary confinement. To be sure, Rosie allowed me between her legs often enough, as I attempted to tunnel to freedom. But there was no future in it; my wife annihilated the sticky traces with spermicide, while I shrank snail-like back into my shell. Strangely, it was not then that I went to pieces, but after the greatest success of my life.

I did not leave my employment empty-handed. Clandestinely, in the slack periods between campaigns, I put together a book for children, based upon the tales that had once entertained my wife. Its title was *Gnomonic Projection*. I cannot show you any of the pictures. But would you be interested in a brief summary of the text?

It started with the supposition that there was, in highest Switzerland, a chocolate factory. And in that factory was the mould from which all chocolate gnomes were made. Naturally, many gnomes denied its existence and maintained that their creation was due to a series of fortuitous accidents. Let's be fair, who could blame them? Hence my first illustration, a portrait of a smile, based on the gnomic aphorism: 'All our lives are mocked by teeth.' As for the majority of gnomes, they inherited the sunny disposition of the cacao bean, and believed in reincarnation. They saw a future beyond the sticky lips of a child.

Gnu, my hero, only half-believed in the chocolate factory. He was a milk-chocolate gnome in the age of plain chocolate. It was a bad time for the paler gnomes. They were not allowed to mix with darker gnomes, some of whose bitterest leaders demanded that all paler gnomes should be melted down. Gangs of plain-chocolate gnomes would attack their milky brothers, who shrugged their shoulders or became cynics. These were accused of undermining pure gnomic culture with alien doubts. Something of a doubter, Gnu decided to address his question to the chocolate-maker himself. Imagine the difficulty a chocolate gnome, only six inches tall, would have in making such a journey! But Gnu was determined, and his courage made him immortal. Open your dictionary. A few words after the entry for *gnome* is something called *gnomonic projection*. This was Gnu's invention. Gnu drew a lot of spheres and tangents and globes and wished very hard. Before he knew what was happening he was in Switzerland! Here Gnu had many adventures. He rescued a mouse from the Gruyère caverns, pulled a spider from the path of a runaway ski and prevented a pretty cow from choking on her own bell and chain. As luck would have it, this was one of the holy cows who supplied the chocolate factory with milk. Of course she was sworn to secrecy, but Gnu had saved her life … High on a peak, across the magic valley, Gnu saw the answer to his question. Even at that distance the air was full of the odours of honey, cacao and milk. A Shangri-la for gnomes? Or the Promised Land? Here's a postscript that I omitted from the book: Gnu found an answer, but lost his question, nor did he find happiness. I dedicated it to Rosie.

Fanfares announced the publication of *Gnomonic Projection*. Even more amazing was its reception: praise, sales, prizes. Such luck! Now I am not so foolish as to believe in retribution, but I am convinced that for every moment of pleasure fate expects a contribution. In short, I was quaking in my boots, waiting for the furies to collect their subscription.

Our one-room apartment faced Hyde Park. Hour after hour I sat in front of the french windows looking down the Bayswater Road in search of the germanic hoards that were coming to invade my body. It happens that the Bayswater Road is one of London's traditional routes for demonstrations, so I was often needlessly alarmed by marchers protesting against nuclear weapons, communism, fascism, unemployment or immigrants. I should have known that the viruses, when they came, would come as thieves in the night. They slipped into our bedroom and sweet-talked their way into my body where my quisling organs welcomed them. On winged heels the ribonucleic acid carried the message: long live the revolution! Proletarian proteins, inflamed by the oratory, burst out of their cells. Pyrexia. Acrophobia. Agoraphobia. Claustrophobia. Viruses X, Y and Z. All teamed up to topple me. It was a tug of war. All my bones were tensed, all my muscles flexed. Then they let go. Crashing backwards I hit a wall and slid to the ground.

When the ambulance men arrived I was staggering around the room, so that they asked my wife, 'Is he under the influence?' They drove me around the corner to St Mary's. I had lost my body, not my mind. As we approached the gates I read the blue plaque that recorded Sir Alexander Fleming's discovery of penicillin in a second-floor room of that very hospital. The fools! They were taking me to the wrong place; everyone knows that antibiotics are only effective against bacteria. Undisturbed, my organs established a puppet government.

It turned out that I had a benign tumour on my adrenal gland, which should have vanished in the embryonic stage of my development. Rather late in the day they removed it, to no avail. My blood pressure remained astronomically high. A pretty nurse tried to relax me with anecdotes about her love-life, but as soon as she tightened the cuff around my arm I felt the triumphant march of my enemies throbbing through my arteries. So they tranquillized me and sent me home.

With the royalties from *Gnomonic Projection* my wife had purchased a small house in the Vale of Health. Perhaps the name was prophetic, or perhaps the pills were working. Clorazepate dipotassium is a light yellow powder. Its structural formula resembles a cockroach with two heads. Before I had a chance to protest I had been colonized by that freakish beetle. 'Eat!' it ordered. I ate. 'Move your bowels once a day,' it commanded. 'No more, no less.' I obeyed. 'Forget everything you ever knew,' it demanded. I became a child again.

One evening I told my wife I was going for a walk on Hampstead Heath and did not return. All summer long I wandered. It was strangely hot. The grass turned brown. At nights it smelled of hay. My hair grew wildly, my beard reached my chest, as if my inner turmoil had been externalized. The only people who sought my company were young thugs who tried to illuminate my mind with the assistance of paraffin and matches. But I was under the protection of the two-headed beetle. Only once was the grip of its pincers nearly loosened.

Day-dreaming opposite Whitestone Pond, I was aroused by the arrival of an ambulance. I identified it as such even though it was marked with a *mogen david* rather than a red cross. My suspicions were confirmed when the occupant of the vehicle, who looked like my grandfather, began to accost certain joggers. Some agreed to place a piece of cloth upon their crowns and wrap small boxes around their forehead and left arms, while the medic compared their readings with those in a small black manual. As if an electrode had been connected to my own skull, certain brainwaves began to hum and an invisible hand squeezed my left arm. Panic-stricken despite my morning Tranxene, I staggered over to the ambulance driver and gasped:

'Take my blood pressure, too!'

'What are you talking about?' he replied. 'These are phylacteries.'

I rummaged among an arcane vocabulary – diastolic, systolic, stethoscope, sphygmomanometer – but could find no trace of phylacteries. Then the runner who was wearing the contraptions cried out, as if he had been struck.

'Jonah!' he exclaimed. 'What's happened to you? Have you even forgotten what *tefilin* look like?' He looked familiar. As did his sweatshirt, marked 'Wingate Football Club'. 'Your wife has been worried sick,' he added.

Having completed the blessings he returned the phylacteries to their owner, who was delighted by the chance reunion his intervention had brought about.

'You see,' he crowed, 'you never know when a *mitzvah* will lead to a miracle.' What was going on?

The footballer gripped me by the arm. 'Come, Jonah,' he said. 'We'll have you back in goal in no time.'

Typographers, beware the printer's devil, 'goal', not 'gaol'. Unfortunately, I heard the latter and fled for my life.

Autumnal air always smells lightly charred as if Nature were organizing its own funeral games. This year the bittersweet aroma arrived very early. And from my vantage point on the Heath I watched London burn. To the north the suburbs of Golders Green and Hendon were put to the torch by bands of black-shirted skinheads. Vengeance was in their hearts, there was no artistry in their dead souls. To the south the banks were ransacked by revolutionaries, clones of the dictators whose faces they wore on their lapels. The east glowed red as blacks battled with police. And in the west turn-coat butlers served molotov cocktails in the casinos and the mansions of the aristocrats and the parvenus. Thanks to gnomonic projection I was omnipresent, for the city was myself. Dead cells were everywhere, as the virus ran rampant. Grey shadows flitted among the smouldering ruins. I floated down streets flowing with blood. There were my kidneys, distributing propaganda and lies. There was my liver, haranguing the masses, making their blood boil. My heart rocked back and forth, like a Jew at prayer.

'Why are you weeping?' I asked.

He looked at me with tear-filled eyes. 'For you,' he replied.

Above it all hovered a burnished figure that shimmered in the glow of the blazing city. His helmet was silver, his body was glass, mercury filled his veins.

Ashkenazia

Many of my fellow-countrymen do not believe in the existence of God. I am more modest. I do not believe in myself. What proof can I have when no one reads what I write? There you have it; my words are the limit of my world. You will therefore smile at this irony; I have been commissioned by our government to write the official English-language *Guide to Ashkenazia*. A guide to *where*? Pick up an atlas. Can you point out Ashkenazia? Don't be embarrassed. The only time we have been news in the last sixty years is when Simcha Nisref won the Nobel Prize for Literature. This gave our Ministry of Culture ideas about its station. Not only has it financed the first International Conference in Yiddish Language and Literature, which opens at the Jagellonian University tomorrow, it has also decided to put Ashkenazia on the map. This is my task: *Fiat Ashkenazia*! Copies of the *Guide* will be placed in the room of every delegate. Including Jake Tarnopol's.

Jake Tarnopol, novelist; notorious, American. It was on account of him that I agreed to write the *Guide* in the first place. This was a calculated sacrifice. In exchange for an introduction to Jake Tarnopol I have lost my good name. My colleagues in the Writers' Circle now refer to me as 'Nisref's lapdog'. They are all jealous of Nisref, of course. But who can blame them? Nisref, alone, has been translated into English. Yiddish is the womb in which the rest of us are trapped, nameless babblers of the *mamaloshen*. Meaning it as a compliment, a critic in the *Forverts* recently called my latest novel 'Tarnopolian'. What fame, to be an adjective! When I buttonhole my qualifier I will beg him to sponsor my publication in America. In America I will be somebody!

Today is Independence Day. Dioramas on open trucks give a panorama of Ashkenazia's achievements, though the inebriated and over-dressed crowds are a more realistic representation of our national potential as producers and consumers of vodka and textiles. However, our most valuable asset is not mentioned in the *Guide*; my paragraph on our uranium deposits was overstamped CENSORED. This is not surprising. Yesterday, knowing there would be no newspapers on a national holiday, our Prime Minister made an unannounced visit to Berlin where he concluded a secret deal with Chancellor Hitler. If the news leaked out that he had sold our uranium to the Germans there would be pandemonium. Let me tell you something else that isn't in the *Guide*; our fear of Germany. Not many of my fellow-citizens take much stock in God, but we all worry about Hitler. Of course we wouldn't be a nation at all if it wasn't for Germany, something Hitler would like to amend if his words are to be believed. After the Great War we were granted autonomy, along with the Armenians and the Kurds, in a sub-clause of the Treaty of Versailles. Five years later we seceded from Poland altogether and declared ourselves an independent state. Poland was weak, Russia was in the middle of a civil war, Germany was ruined. We survived. Then Germany elected Hitler. Half our politicians believe that Hitler should be placated, the other half that he should be outfaced. Since the majority of our people favour a quiet life the former have prevailed. But we have our prophets.

Perhaps you've read Nisref's latest novel, *Wawel*? It starts with the premise that Britain and France threw Czechoslovakia (another creation of Versailles) to the dogs at Munich. What follows is a terrible vision. Having overrun the Continent the Germans turn their attention to Ashkenazia. Here Nisref reworks an ancient legend. Cracow – our capital city – is dominated by a limestone hill, Wawel. Today it is topped by a castle, hitherto it was the domain of a fire-breathing dragon. In order to build the castle, which was required to defend the city, the dragon had to be appeased. So the ruler drove scores of his subjects into the dragon's cave where they were incinerated and devoured. This is the inspiration of *Operation Wawel*, Hitler's code name for the destruction of Ashkenazia and its people. Nisref turns the dismemberment of our name – a nation burnt to *ashes* by the *nazis* – into a metaphor for our fate. Needless to say, *Wawel* provoked an outcry in Ashkenazia. It was branded obscene, the morbid fantasies of a madman. Hitler was not amused either. He threatened to visit Ashkenazia in person and destroy every copy of the book. Instead our Prime Minister went to Berlin.

He returns from his latest visit in time to open the conference. A crowd has gathered outside the university to greet him. As the Prime Minister walks up the steps towards the great oak doors, a lone demonstrator dressed in a dragon-skin pelts him with mushrooms. A smudged leaflet explains that the mushrooms symbolize the atomic bombs Germany will build from our uranium. My comrades in the Writers' Circle are convinced that the man is a hired lackey, paid by

Nisref to publicize *Wawel*. Such is the informed gossip as we jostle one another in an attempt to find the secretary whose job is to match us with the badges that bear our names.

'Clement Stashev,' she cries.

'Here,' I say.

'Olga Stashev,' says my wife. But so indecent is her dress she can find nowhere to pin her tag.

Have I mentioned my wife? The daughter of an Ashkenazi man and an English Jewess, which gives her certain advantages; above all, she is bilingual. In fact she is one of our top translators, presently competing for this year's plum: Jake Tarnopol's latest – *Dreams After Death*. Meanwhile, she has just completed translating my novel into English – all my English is fit for is the *Guide to Ashkenazia*. Her fee? A meeting with Tarnopol. Olga is also a journalist, with a weekly column in *Forverts*. Once she wrote about two dogs, but the disguise was transparent. One dog barked all day, the other learned the language of humans; while the former was more original, the latter earned the money. This was sufficient for my colleagues to dub me 'Olga's poodle'. Of course my wife is correct, translators are more important than writers in Ashkenazia. But in America I will be the celebrity. Fools! See how they ogle Olga as we take our seats in the auditorium My accomplished wife.

The great hall is full. The important guests – including Jake Tarnopol – sit in the front row. We – the writers of Ashkenazia – sit at the back. Simcha Nisref is on the platform between the Minister of Culture and the Prime Minister. The theme of the Premier's opening speech is 'The Renaissance in Yiddish Literature'. Our Leonardo is Simcha Nisref, of course, but who are the young lions? Every neck in the back row cranes forward to catch the names, our ears make ready to burn. What madmen we are! Is the Prime Minister our public relations officer? He is not interested in us, he is only here to heap praises upon the already famous. So it's Simcha Nisref this, and Simcha Nisref that. While the applause is still crackling Nisref walks to the podium.

' "I would tell you, ladies and gentlemen," ' he begins, ' "how much better you understand Yiddish than you suppose." Not my words, but Kafka's. So what did he mean? I'll explain. Yiddish is the language of the heart, the heart is informed by suffering, suffering is Esperanto.

If you listen with your heart you will understand. There is a Yiddish proverb which states: "The heart is half a prophet". Our hearts tell us the consequences of every action, they can see into the future. Now the world has begun to listen to us at last – let us pray it is not too late. Friends, the Nobel Prize was for Yiddish Literature, not for Simcha Nisref. Fellow writers, seize the time!'

At which point my wife rises so quickly that her breasts flop in and out of her dress. Nisref, old though he is, stares gleefully.

'You're nothing but a *pornographnik*!' Olga shouts. 'Your stories are not filled with love of humanity but with fear of women. If – God forbid – we enjoy sex, we are in league with the devil. Have any of you read *Wawel* properly? To me Hitler is merely the agent of retribution, the angel of death. The real culprit is the Prime Minister's mistress. So what has Nisref got against women? Believe me, it has nothing to do with religion or philosophy, but everything to do with vanity. You know that I am one of Nisref's translators, but that is not enough for the old goat, there are other services he requires. "Come swimming with me in the Vistula," he begged. Like a fool, I agreed. He took me into the country, to an empty stretch of the river. "Here we can swim without costumes," he said. I am a married woman; I refused.'

The wives of my fellow writers can contain themselves no longer, their titters evolve into fits of giggling. The husbands – cuckolds every one – fill the hall with their hoots of derision. They are laughing at me, and I am red with shame. I do not like to admit this, but I am also jealous. I dread what is coming next.

'Nisref had no such qualms,' continues Olga, 'down came his trunks. "Touch it," he pleaded. Touch that thing! It was dark and shrivelled and covered with scabs of dry skin that looked like parchment. "Please," he said. "If you do I'll introduce your husband to my American publisher." I couldn't believe my ears. I turned and ran. In short, Nisref hates women because we find him repulsive.'

Press photographers are fighting to get a close-up of my wife's bosom. Thanks to them, the stewards cannot get near enough to evict her. 'Sit down,' I hiss, 'or I'll strangle you.'

'Why are you so upset?' says Olga. 'Because I didn't tell you about it before, or because I didn't get your book published in America?'

Forget me, what about Nisref? Thank God he doesn't look too upset. And the Prime Minister is beaming. With reason. He knows that tomorrow's front pages will be filled with pictures of Olga. The protest against his secret deal with Germany will be forgotten. My wife resumes her seat. The treacherous bitch!

Only Olga would have the gall to show herself at the Prime Minister's reception after a performance like that. Her presence casts a shadow over my triumph. Alone among the younger members of the Writers' Circle I have an official invitation – signed by the Minister of Culture himself. You should have seen their faces when I strolled past the doorman. Green. Now where is Tarnopol? I have suffered much for this moment. First, the *Guide*. Then, this morning: the Prime Minister's banalities, my wife's disgraceful exhibition, and an interminable paper on the origins of Yiddish. The woman who delivered it said she was a 'structuralist'. Since no one really knows where Yiddish began, she had to construct a country whose language she called 'Proto-Yiddish'. To what purpose? So she would have a constant reference for the divergent forms of modern Yiddish, and know at once whether we in Cracow who say *strafn* are greater deviants than those in Lublin who say *strufn*.

But I must not mock. Any discipline which considers history an irrelevant nuisance cannot be all bad. There she is, deep in conversation with the Prime Minister. And why not? Politics is a form of structuralism, after all. So is writing guide-books. Nisref joins the Prime Minister. I listen.

'Is what I hear true,' he asks, 'that you have sold our uranium to Germany?'

'Maybe, maybe not,' says the Prime Minister. 'But I'll tell you this: Hitler hates communists more than he hates Jews. In Russia we have a common enemy. This is all I need to know. I am a politician, not a philosopher.'

'You are a fool,' replies Nisref.

'You want to know the truth?' says the Prime Minister. 'I'll tell you. It became necessary to pay for our survival.'

'With our souls!' cries Nisref. 'You have paid protection money to the devil. Must we have a catastrophe every generation? Is this what it means to be the chosen people? Mark my words, your deal with Germany will bring destruction to Ashkenazia.'

Suddenly I am faced with a bigger problem than the Prime Minister; how to construct a conversation with Nisref's wife. She is approaching fast.

'Olga,' I whisper, 'make yourself scarce.'

'Don't be an idiot,' she replies.

'My dear,' says Nisref's wife. 'I must thank you. The old fool was beginning to think he'd become irresistible to women. Perhaps your little revelation has brought him to his senses.'

Tarnopol, too, wants to praise my wife.

'Do you know Freud?' he asks. 'Well, he maintained that writing is motivated by a wish to attract members of the opposite sex. He hit the nail on the head in my case. My desire to write coincided with puberty. I celebrated the publication of my first story with my first ever fuck. And the more I published the more I got laid, until I ended up married to a *Vogue* cover-girl. Now I have to write to pay off her alimony. Some joke; my winged muse has become my albatross. What a country! Have you visited America?'

What a question! Would we be here now if we'd ever made it to America?

'Instant gratification,' says Tarnopol, 'that's America. A cowboy drives his herd into the kitchen, and five minutes later a beautiful waitress is serving us hamburgers in our automobiles. And as for desserts – we have one hundred and fifty different flavours of ice-cream to choose from.'

His eyes are scoops, my wife's breasts the flavour of the month. But don't flatter yourself, Tarnopol. It's not on account of your looks that she's all over you. A balding Jew approaching middle age is no one's idea of physical beauty.

'You'd be a big hit in America,' says Tarnopol, 'you remind me of Jane Fonda.'

'Ah, Jane Fonda,' says Olga, flattered. 'She has courage. Just what we lack in Ashkenazia. Oh, we mock the authorities behind their backs. Do you know why our police force is called the "militcia"? Because we measure intelligence in "cias" and a thousandth of a "cia" is ... But as a nation we cut our cloth to fit our needs.'

Clearly, the cut of Olga's cloth suits Tarnopol down to the ground, so much so that he alters the place-cards in the banqueting hall to be beside her at dinner.

Here, finally, he asks: 'What do you do?'

'My husband is a writer,' replies Olga, 'and I am a translator.'

'In that case,' he says, 'I hope you are not responsible for the English version of the menu: "Boiled Buttock of Beef, Sterilized String Beans, Bags filled with Plum Jam." Not very appetizing.'

'That was the work of our state translators,' says Olga, 'a bunch of fools. I translate literature. To tell you the truth, I am hoping to translate *Dreams After Death* into Yiddish.'

Tarnopol laughs. 'If your work's good – it's yours,' he says. 'Bring some examples to my hotel tomorrow – before lunch.'

I love my wife.

The man at the Hotel Rambam's reception desk tells Olga that Tarnopol is out. She ignores him and goes straight to Tarnopol's room.

Tarnopol does not recognize her. 'I'm sorry,' he says, 'I was expecting someone else.'

'I'll go,' says Olga.

'Please,' he says, 'let me explain. When I opened the door I thought I would see my grandfather's ghost. This morning I strolled down to the Kazimierz district to take a look at the old synagogues. Well, I'm ready to return when I see this hasidic type staring at me. He looks familiar. "*Jacob, mein klein Jacob*," he whispers. It's my grandfather. Who is dead. I panic. He follows me back to the hotel. There is a knock on my door. Instead of my grandfather's ghost a beautiful woman is standing there. Perhaps you can appreciate my confusion. The strangest thing is that today is the anniversary of my grandfather's death. Look, I even brought an electric *yortzeit* from America to burn for him.' Tarnopol points to a small glass in which flickers an imitation flame. 'What more can he want?'

'Perhaps he wants his freedom, like the rest of us,' says Olga. 'Sometimes I think we are all ghosts in Ashkenazia. We do not live in the twentieth century, but in a timeless zone. Figments of your imagination. Perhaps your grandfather is sick of being your conscience. You want our burdens, we want your freedoms. Can't we do a deal?' Olga hands him her translation of my novel.

'I must ask you something in return,' Tarnopol replies.

Early next morning, as we drive towards the Hotel Rambam, we are forced off the road by a speeding fire-engine. The Rambam itself is swarming with firemen. Smoke is pouring from one of the upper windows. Like a heavenly choir the guests in their white night-clothes stand in a group answering when the receptionist calls their names. Only one is missing.

'I can't be certain,' says Olga, 'but I think the smoke is coming from Jake's room.'

Sure enough Tarnopol's face appears at the cracked and sooty window-pane. *O God*, I pray, *don't let my saviour be burnt to a cinder*. Like the angel who rescued the Jews from the fiery furnace a fireman rises on a ladder that is pointing towards Tarnopol's room. Thereafter the rescue is rapid. Tarnopol is brought to the ground slung over the fireman's shoulder. He is not only breathing but coughing.

'What happened?' I ask.

'I nearly died, that's all,' Tarnopol replies. 'I was asleep. Dreaming about my grandfather, of course. I was a little boy and he had come into my room to tuck me in. Only he kept pulling the blanket over my face. "*Schlof, mein kind*," he hummed. Lucky for me I always was a disobedient brat. I woke up. Otherwise I would have suffocated in my sleep. Hey! You don't think my grandfather was trying to murder me, do you?'

Later I ask a fireman: 'Have you found the cause of the fire?'

'You won't believe this,' he replies, 'but it was started by a short circuit in that electric *yortzeit* of his.' He laughs 'What will the Americans think of next?'

Though Tarnopol feels he is the victim of a gross injustice he is full of remorse.

'I wanted to do right by my grandfather,' he says. 'I wanted to let his memorial light burn twenty-four hours like the rabbis tell you. I thought an electric *yortzeit* would be safer than a candle in a glass. How was I supposed to know it was dangerous to run it off the current you have in Ashkenazia?'

'Forget it,' says Olga, 'let's save what we can of the day.'

'But what about that manuscript you left with me?' he says. 'You know it was destroyed, don't you?'

Olga nods.

'I only read a few chapters,' he says, 'but it had real quality. You'll have to let me make good your loss. Name your price.'

'We'll think of something,' I say. Actually we have a copy, but why spoil his guilt? America, here we come!

To be more accurate we are driving in our imported Polski Fiat towards the town of Tarnopol, eponymous birthplace of the unquiet grandfather. It's a fair exchange; we take Tarnopol back to his past, he takes us into our future; we show each other what our lives might have been. Every few miles we stop so that the American can take a photograph. The countryside of Ashkenazia is at its most beautiful in the late summer, when the farmers are in the swaying fields gathering their harvest. Although we have been cut adrift from the historical process, the seasonal cycle keeps us in tune with a more fundamental motion. The rhythms of which are so perfect that they all but lull you into a belief in God. Who else could create such harmony? But the farmers put no trust in divinity; indeed they mock it, with their humanoid haystacks built upon skeletons of wood. Nor do they put their faith in modern inventions. They travel by horse and cart. Sometimes they wave as we speed past. It is a humid day, full of clouds and showers.

Passing through one such downpour we roll up the windows so that condensation quickly obscures the windscreen, revealing also a message written with a fingertip: 'I do love you.' By whom? To whom? Is it just the ghost of a forgotten night with Olga? Or the echo of a guilty secret? Does she have a lover? My unfathomable wife. The words hover over my horizon for a few moments, until they are blown away by the de-mister. By the time we reach Tarnopol the sun is shining, and there is not a cloud in the sky.

After the rain, now in the sun, Tarnopol looks like a town built upon hot coals. Steam rises from the open sewers in picturesque tendrils, so densely in the back streets that the hasidim there do not seem to have their feet upon the ground at all. The boys are happy, jumping the puddles; but some of the young men in their greasy gaberdines look broken-hearted, sentenced to a life of unimaginative solipsism, banished forever from America.

'Behold, your brothers,' I say.

Tarnopol, the man, two generations removed, is aghast. He jumps in fear as a black-garbed ancient grabs his arm and tugs him towards a dilapidated synagogue. 'Be a good Jew,' he says. 'Perform a *mitzvah*, say a prayer for your grandfather's soul.'

Poor Jake! His tongue shrinks, his face turns bloodless; he is struck dumb, he faints. Olga unbuttons his shirt. She sprinkles eau-de-cologne upon his forehead.

'Ashkenazia is not for you,' she says, 'it is too ugly.' She is right; Tarnopol past is more than Tarnopol future can take. He opens his eyes.

'I'm sorry,' he says, 'it must be the after-effects of all that smoke I inhaled this morning.' Cured of his sentimental atavism, it is Jake's turn to take revenge.

121

'If only Tarnopol didn't really exist,' he says.

We stop half-way to Cracow for a picnic supper. The field we choose is full of stacks of drying grass that look like *golem* awaiting the breath of life. Our food is in the shadow, we are in the sun. I remove my jacket. Tarnopol digs his fingers into the earth, as if making one last effort to root them. We break the bread and crumble the cheese. Some curious cows wander towards us, coloured black and white, like the world view of the hasidim. A slight breeze carries a foul stench from their direction. As I run, waving my arms, to shoo them away, I see the source of the bad air: one of the creatures has a hole in its side, punched by its owner, out of which pumps a bright green fluid that looks as poisonous as it smells. Chasing the offensive cow into the neighbouring field I feel I am shaking off my previous persona – even Ashkenazia itself – which also was in danger of exploding from an overflow of gall. But no longer. Thanks to Jake Tarnopol, who is just about to give me horns.

An unnatural gust of wind catches the stack behind which we were sitting and disperses it in a bilious dance to reveal Olga and Tarnopol copulating like animals. Caught out, the guilty man spills his seed upon Ashkenazia's soil. Is that who we are – the children of Onan? You throw out the old values, turn your back for a second, and look what happens! My heart is in my mouth.

'Slut!' I scream.

Olga, though naked, is unruffled.

'What are you so upset about?' she says. 'Don't tell me you've never imagined doing it with another woman. As far as I am concerned anticipation makes you as guilty as participation. Any attempt to resist temptation is merely hypocrisy.'

A hypocrite my polluted wife is not; she refuses to cover herself, unlike Tarnopol who kneels with his hand over his privates.

'You're wrong, Olga,' I say, 'there is all the difference in the world between wanting and doing. Hitler might want to kill me, but I'll only be upset if he does. Thoughts are harmless; deeds are like demons let loose on earth. Once free there is no knowing what havoc they will cause. Already they are whispering in my ear, "Divorce her, or better yet – kill her." And why not? Isn't the most terrible implication of infidelity the contemplation of eternal loss? Translated into words your actions say, "I am prepared to risk never seeing you again." You and Tarnopol have created a world in which I do not exist. Now we must await the consequences.'

They are not long in coming, though who was to blame – Olga, Tarnopol, or the Prime Minister – historians will have to decide.

Suddenly we are engulfed by puffs of hot air as summer vanishes and the seasons accelerate. Hurricanes tear the haystacks apart. Blades of grass rip into us like green rain. Hail becomes a blizzard. We tumble to the ground and the grass piles around us until we are buried. The wind dies. I return from the grave. But Olga and Tarnopol look like fallen haystacks. Neither mound moves. Great mushrooms are growing in the sky. Flames lick the horizon as though Wawel's dragon were once again stalking the land. All that remains of my dumb heart-broken country is a field of wooden skeletons.

Now the world will listen to me, for I am the guide to Ashkenazia. I am Ashkenazia!